'He married you f...

At first Alexi thought she had misheard him. She frowned, completely at a loss. 'Revenge? Henri, I don't understand you. What possible reason would Max have to hate me that much?' She almost felt like laughing with relief as she asked the question. The idea was too ludicrous to have any truth in it.

'He hates you because you are my daughter.'

Dear Reader

The summer holidays are now behind us—but Mills & Boon still have lots of treats in store for you! Why not indulge yourself in long, romantic evenings by the fire? We're sure you'll find our heroes simply irresistible! And perhaps you'd like to experience the exotic beauty of the Bahamas—or the glamour of Milan? Whatever you fancy, just curl up with this month's selection of enchanting love stories—and let your favourite authors carry you away!

Happy reading!

The Editor

Kathryn Ross was born in Zambia where her parents happened to live at that time. Educated in Ireland and England, she now lives in a village near Blackpool, Lancashire. Kathryn is a professional beauty therapist, but writing is her first love. As a child she wrote adventure stories and at thirteen was editor of her school magazine. Happily, ten writing years later, *Designed with Love* was accepted by Mills & Boon. A romantic Sagittarian, she loves travelling to exotic locations.

Recent titles by the same author:

BY LOVE ALONE

TOTAL POSSESSION

BY
KATHRYN ROSS

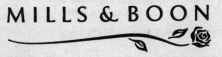

MILLS & BOON

MILLS & BOON LIMITED
ETON HOUSE, 18-24 PARADISE ROAD
RICHMOND, SURREY TW9 1SR

To Harry and Irene Ingham
and fond memories of the
Napa Valley.

*First published in Great Britain 1993
by Mills & Boon Limited*

© Kathryn Ross 1993

*Australian copyright 1993
Philippine copyright 1993
This edition 1993*

ISBN 0 263 78263 8

*Set in Times Roman 10 on 11¼ pt.
01-9311-55749 C*

Made and printed in Great Britain

CHAPTER ONE

THE large mansion in Beverly Hills was ablaze with lights. Another party for the rich and famous was in full swing.

The parking area at the front of the house was full and the long driveway was now lined with gleaming Rolls-Royces, Jaguars, Porsches, cars that spoke of wealth and success, each with a personalised number-plate. The plates read like a list of credits for an Academy-award-winning film, Alexandra thought as her Lamborghini swept past them, hardly surprising when that was exactly what everyone had come to celebrate.

She managed to find a space around the side of the Georgian-style manor and climbed out into the warmth of the summer evening. She locked the shiny black sports car and dropped the keys into her Chanel handbag as she waited for her escort for the evening to walk around from the passenger side to join her.

'Feeling better now?' Miles Thornton smiled down at her and she nodded.

'Well, you certainly look good.' Grey eyes swept appraisingly over her slender figure. 'Although you have lost a little too much weight recently,' he added cautiously.

'My father will be pleased. He's always telling me I need to lose some weight,' Alexandra said with a wry smile.

'Nonsense. There was nothing of you to start with.' Miles frowned at such stupidity. He didn't care for Alexandra's father. He was a hard man and, in Miles's opinion, unnecessarily tough on his only daughter. 'You're fading away, Alexi; I just wish I could get you to agree to take a holiday.'

Alexandra smiled up at her friend and business partner. He was always very protective towards her; sometimes it felt as if he was the only one around who really cared for her as a person. 'We haven't got time for holidays, Miles, and you know it.'

'I know that you need a rest, Alexi; you've been putting in too many hours,' he said grimly. He held the door open and they walked in to the grandeur of the spacious hallway. A maid took Alexandra's silk wrap, and Miles thought once more how fragile his friend looked.

'It's all my fault that you've been overdoing things,' he murmured now. 'I've been taking too much time off since Nancy started to be ill.'

'That is nonsense, Miles; your wife has needed you these past couple of weeks and I've coped perfectly well.'

'You always cope perfectly.' He smiled. 'But I still think it's been too much for you.' His eyes moved over her slender figure and he felt another pang of guilt. She really had been over-working recently and then on top of that there had been all this publicity about the breakup of her relationship with screen idol Martin Steel.

She looked like a fragile china figurine in the long white Grecian-style dress. Her thick long dark hair gave dramatic emphasis to the porcelain-pale skin. At twenty-eight years of age, Alexandra Rossini was a highly desirable young woman. Not only was she the epitome of true classical beauty, she was also heiress to a large fortune. Her father was none other than Henri Rossini, one of the most powerful and influential men in Hollywood.

'It would do you a world of good to get out from under the spotlight for a couple of weeks,' Miles murmured now, almost to himself.

She grinned up at him mischievously. 'But think how good the spotlight is for the business. The more the media focus attention on us, the more people ring the agency asking for us to come out and redesign their houses.'

'Nonsense. They ask you to come out because you are one of the most talented, sought-after interior designers in the area.'

Alexandra said nothing to that. She was good at her job, she knew that, but she was also a realist. She knew the success their business was enjoying had a lot to do with her name and her connections...namely her father.

You were considered to have made it when you moved into a house in the 'right area' of Beverly Hills, and if you had Alexi Rossini dropping by to put an eye over the inside of the house you had really made it to the big time. The Alexi-Miles design studio was something of a status symbol; a hostess liked nothing better than to mention casually that she had just commissioned them to go over the place. But what was considered a hot success one day could be, 'Not quite the thing, darling,' the next. Alexi knew that, so did Miles; that was one of the reasons they drove themselves so hard, ploughing most of their money and all of their energy back into the business.

They moved through into the lounge. The sound of a small orchestra playing Vivaldi filtered through the open patio doors from the pool area. It was the title track of the new film, another tremendous success to emerge from the stables of Henri Rossini's film studios.

There were about a hundred guests intermingling between the garden area outside and the large lounge. They all looked cool and elegant. The clothes spoke of designer labels, and diamonds flashed fire at the throats of fashionably pallid women.

'We are in for another scintillating evening, I see,' Miles remarked drily.

Alexandra's lips twisted in amusement. Neither of them liked these parties. Only the most successful and the most elite of Hollywood society had received an invitation. People came for no other reason than to see and be seen as one of the successful, beautiful people. Before the evening was over a few deals would be struck, and hopefully the Alexi-Miles agency would be extra busy next week. 'We'll circulate and sparkle with the stars for a while, then make a discreet exit, shall we?' she suggested in a low tone.

'I was hoping you would say that; not that I don't love these parties.' Miles smiled sardonically. He was a good-looking man in his late thirties, his hair steel-grey, his eyes a smoky lighter colour. 'I am a bit worried about Nancy, though,' he added more seriously. 'She still looks so ill. If we hadn't felt this party was important I would never have left her this evening.'

Alexandra nodded. She had felt quite concerned herself when she had seen Miles's wife. She had looked washed-out, completely unlike her usual bubbly self. 'You should have let me come on my own; I told you I wouldn't have minded.'

'I know you wouldn't. But you need some moral support at the moment.' A waiter came over and Miles took two glasses of champagne from the tray and handed her one. 'I couldn't leave you alone with these vultures,' he whispered against her ear.

She laughed. 'Unfortunately I'm well used to the vultures, having been raised and brought up in their midst. I could even be described as one of them.'

Miles shook his head. 'Oh, no, Alexi. Anyone who really knows you knows you don't belong in that circle. I realise you will never admit it, and you put on a hell of a good show of being as tough as the rest of them, but you're as vulnerable as a babe around this lot.'

Before Alexandra had a chance to make any reply to that, their hostess for the evening came across to greet them.

'Alexi, darling, how wonderful to see you.' Penelope James looked extremely attractive in the floating Dior silk. No one would ever have guessed that the youthful, slender figure and the high cheekbones belonged to a woman of nearly fifty. Her blonde hair sat perfectly in a silken bob, and the blue eyes that swept upwards towards Miles were an incredible shade of blue.

Penelope spent every spare moment at the beauty salons and the health studios working out. There were rumours that she had also undergone a tremendous amount of surgery, all in an attempt to keep her handsome husband, Robert James, who was one of the most sought-after actors in Hollywood.

'Isn't Nancy with you?' she asked Miles curiously.

'She isn't too well, Penelope. So I'm afraid I won't be able to stay long. Just wanted to pop in and congratulate Robert.'

'Yes, I'm so proud of him. This is his second Oscar, you know. He received one for his performance in *Sergeant Thomas*. Shame your father couldn't be here tonight, Alexi,' she continued on without hardly a pause for breath.

'Yes. He flew out to England directly after the Oscar ceremony. He's shooting a new film over there,' Alexandra informed her unnecessarily. Everyone knew where her father was; everyone knew about the new film.

'Well, never mind,' Penelope went on blithely. 'We'll have another little celebration for him when he gets back.'

Another little celebration being about three hundred guests, Alexi guessed drily.

'I was sorry to hear that you and Martin have split up, Alexi.' Sharp blue eyes homed in on her now. 'I always thought you two were made for each other.'

'We're still good friends, Penny.' Alexandra noted wryly how the woman made it sound as if they had been living together for years, when in fact she had only dated Martin for a few months. 'He's going to be in England for a while, that's all.'

'Yes, of course, darling,' the other woman purred soothingly. 'I read about it in the papers. Your father offered him the lead in his new film. I must say I was rather surprised that he had given that part to such a young actor. I would have thought that Robert would have been more suited to it.' She shrugged slim shoulders and then gave a silvery false laugh. 'But Henri must know what he's doing.'

Of course Henri Rossini knew what he was doing. He had succeeded in separating Martin Steel from his daughter. A most unsatisfactory match in his opinion, and Henri always expressed his opinions very forcefully and very openly. It was no wonder the scandal papers had got wind of the real reason Martin Steel had been offered such a part.

'Well, do excuse me, darling.' Penelope cast her eyes towards the door where some more people were entering. 'I must go and greet my guests. Do help yourselves to the buffet; it's through by the patio. I had that little catering firm Harper and Jones do it, and I must say it really is superb.'

Miles rolled his eyes heavenwards as she departed. 'Little firm Harper and Jones.' He mimicked her in an outrageously false tone. Everyone knew that the agency she had named was the largest and most prestigious, and that all the 'in' people were hiring them. 'I think I need another drink.' He reached and took another champagne glass from one of the passing waiters. Alexi shook her head as the tray was then offered to her.

'They're all so damn false,' Miles muttered in an undertone as he took a sip of his drink.

'Goes with the territory, darling,' Alexi drawled with a laugh. 'You have to put up a front just to survive out here, as you and I both know.' Her eyes travelled around the room and lighted on Penny's husband. He was standing very close to Monica Houston, the young, attractive blonde actress who had co-starred opposite him in his last film. Monica had shot to stardom soon after she had started dating Alexi's father. She now resided at Henri Rossini's mansion.

For a moment Alexandra found herself wondering if the woman was intending to amuse herself with Robert while Henri was out of town. She felt a pang of distaste at the thought and immediately tried to banish it from her mind. Relationships were so transient out here; people were so shallow.

Alexi glanced down at her champagne glass. Growing up in such an environment had been very lonely; sometimes she still felt that loneliness despite her successful business and her friendship with Miles and Nancy.

She glanced up as Miles started to say something else, and her attention was caught and held by a man standing just inside the patio doors. In a room full of Hollywood's most attractive heroes he was the most handsome man she had ever seen, and yet she couldn't put a name to him.

He was probably in his mid-thirties. He was incredibly tall, well over six feet. The dark dinner-jacket he wore emphasised a body that was broad-shouldered, superbly lithe and fit.

Just looking at him made Alexandra catch her breath. Who was that man? She had thought she knew everyone at this party, but she was quite sure she had never met him. His hair had the dark sheen of a raven's wing, his eyes were a brightly piercing flame-blue, and they held hers in a powerfully assessing way that was totally unnerving.

She wrenched her gaze away from him and forced herself to take a sip of champagne before asking Miles in a casual voice, 'There's a man standing over by the patio doors; have you any idea who he is?'

Miles lifted one eyebrow drily, then glanced over discreetly. He shook his head. 'No idea. Must be someone important to warrant an invite; he's talking to Georgia Gold, the columnist, and she seems very intent on his every word.'

Alexandra turned her attention back towards him. She had been so caught up in watching him that she hadn't noticed who he was standing with. Now her eyes moved over the attractive blonde with a certain amount of distaste.

Georgia Gold was nothing more than a scandal-monger and she had written some very distressing things about Alexandra in the past, things that had been a complete distortion of the truth.

The other woman glanced over and caught Alexandra watching her. Vivid scarlet lips curved in a smile that was as false as it was bright. Then she turned her attention back to the handsome stranger. Alexandra had the distinct impression for a second that they were discussing her. If they were, then the man would certainly not like what he heard. Then she dismissed the idea. She was getting paranoid; just because their eyes had met briefly did not mean he was pumping Georgia Gold for information on her.

'Alexi?' Miles's voice brought her attention sharply winging back. 'You haven't heard a word I've just said, have you?' he asked with amusement.

'Sorry... I was miles away,' she murmured, feeling a little embarrassed at being so openly interested in the man opposite.

'I was asking if you had thought about the offer that agency made for your house?'

Alexandra shook her head. 'I'm not going to sell it, Miles, and I don't know why they keep pestering me with offers. It's driving me mad.'

'I think you should consider this one, Alexi,' Miles told her seriously. 'The amount they have offered is staggering. And quite honestly the place is costing a fortune you can ill afford at the moment.'

'I can't sell it, Miles.' There was no indecision in Alexandra's voice. 'It was a gift from my father, and anyway I love the place.'

'OK.' Miles shrugged. 'It's up to you, of course, but I think you should consider that offer for a couple of days before you turn it down.'

'All right, Miles, I'll consider it for two days and then I'll turn it down,' she said with a mischievous grin.

'Hell, you are a stubborn woman. How we manage to work together so successfully I have no idea.' He gave her dark hair an affectionate ruffle, then glanced at his watch. 'Excuse me a moment, honey. I'm just going to give Nancy a quick buzz on the phone to see if she's all right.'

Alexandra nodded. 'Tell her you'll bring her home some pizza to make up for missing the Harper and Jones buffet,' she joked.

'I'm sure that will make her feel a lot better,' Miles said with a laugh as he disappeared in the direction of the entrance hall.

Alexandra turned her head towards the patio doors, but the man she had been watching earlier had gone. She sipped her champagne idly and glanced at the other people around her.

The place was really filling up now. She made her way carefully through the crowds towards the patio doors. Her gaze travelled out across the brightly lit pool towards the dance-floor crammed with couples dancing to a romantic ballad played by the small orchestra.

'Alexandra Rossini, I believe?' The deep voice next to her made her turn, and she found herself looking upwards, directly into those startling flame-blue eyes.

'Yes.' For a moment her mind went blank. She just stared at him. He was so incredibly good-looking. The features were strongly chiselled, the jaw square, his mouth powerfully sensual.

His gaze was also moving over her, taking in the slender lines of her body, the creamy bare neckline, the luxuriously thick hair framing the delicate face and huge green eyes. Curiously there was a cool detachment in the way he was regarding her, quite unlike the way men usually looked at her. It was as if he was weighing her up, assessing her. It gave Alexandra a very strange feeling of foreboding.

'I'm afraid you have an advantage on me. I don't believe we have been introduced.' She hesitated and waited for him to supply his name.

He smiled, a slow, lazy smile that made her pulses quicken. She couldn't remember any man having such a profound effect on her senses. 'That's good. I like starting off with an advantage.' The velvet-smooth tone made a shiver run through her.

'So?' Her eyes were wide and enquiring as she waited for him to enlighten her.

'Max Channing.' His gaze never left her face; he seemed to note every flicker of her eyelashes, every expression in the bright green of her eyes.

'Channing...' The name was familiar; she frowned as she ran it through her memory bank. Then she smiled and her brow cleared. 'Maxwell Channing, owner of the Brightwell film studios in England and a publishing company in New York.'

'Among other things.' He inclined his head. 'Very good, Miss Rossini.'

'I should think that most people have heard of Maxwell Channing,' she murmured. No wonder the man was surrounded by an aura of power. He was on a par with her father, a wheeler-dealer, an astutely clever businessman. She found that the comparison made her feel a little down-hearted. For some strange reason she didn't like to think that this man was used to the power struggles and the ruthless dealings that surrounded her father's life. 'Are you in California on business, Mr Channing?'

'Yes. I've taken a house down on Malibu beach for a while. Perhaps you would like to come out and take a look at it some time?' he invited smoothly.

For a moment there was confusion in her wide eyes. She was unsure as to if that was a personal invitation or an offer of work.

He smiled. 'I was speaking in a professional capacity, of course.'

'Of course.' Now she felt profoundly embarrassed. She realised that she had romantically read a little too much into the way their eyes had met across the room. Even if Maxwell Channing found her attractive, and she was very unsure on that, he was probably married with six children.

'Although we could bring the arrangement around towards something on a little more of a social level,' he went on to suggest casually, while the eyes that moved over her body were anything but casual.

Alexandra frowned. She had the distinct impression that this man was playing with her, that he was testing her out in some way, evaluating her every reaction towards him.

'How social were you planning to get, Mr Channing?' She lifted her chin and met his gaze boldly. She was not a shrinking violet and she wasn't going to allow him to imagine for one moment that he was intimidating her in any way.

He laughed at that. It was a warm sound, and she felt herself relaxing as she listened to it. 'Why, Miss Rossini, I do hope that you aren't misconstruing my intentions.'

'I really don't know, Mr Channing; perhaps you would care to state your intentions more clearly?' She deftly parried the teasing remarks, sending them firmly back at him.

For a moment he was silent. The blue eyes were calm and strangely cool as he pretended to consider the question. 'Let's see, now. I thought dinner tomorrow, followed by lunch and dinner the next day.' One eyebrow lifted in a mocking, quizzical way. 'Followed by breakfast perhaps the next day... Am I going a little too fast for you?'

She kept her features perfectly controlled as she nodded. 'I'm sure that's the speed you usually work at.'

'Yes, I must agree. I don't like to wait around...for anything.' There was a steel-like tone to those words, then he smiled and the effect was humorous again. 'So where was I...? Oh, yes, breakfast...or maybe brunch, depending on what time we get up.' He watched with a certain satisfaction as a little colour crept into her cheeks. 'Then a short engagement followed by a whirlwind wedding.'

Now she laughed, a feeling of relief mingling with her discomfiture at such blatantly tantalising teasing. 'Followed by a divorce, say, two weeks later?'

'Two weeks!' Blue eyes moved heavenwards in horror. 'That's a bit of a lengthy marriage by Hollywood standards, isn't it?'

'I suppose it is.' She gave a wry grin. 'And I only came out to do a bit of decorating.'

He nodded, his features serious. 'If I were you, honey, I'd take the warning and stick to the work schedule.' He paused and then the firm lips twisted into an arrogant smile. 'But how do you feel about dinner tomorrow?'

CHAPTER TWO

BEFORE she could make any reply to the invitation, Miles rejoined her.

'Sorry to interrupt.' He smiled at them both, but there was a worried light in his eyes that did not escape Alexandra's attention.

'This is my friend and business partner, Miles Thornton. Miles, this is Maxwell Channing.' Politely she introduced the two men and watched as they shook hands.

There was a part of her that was glad that Miles had returned when he did; it saved her having to make an immediate reply to that dinner invitation. It wasn't that she didn't want to accept, because she did. It was more the fact that there was a tiny part of her that was afraid of Maxwell Channing. Why on earth he scared her she couldn't understand. She was not a timid person; on the contrary, she was on the whole a self-assured and very outgoing woman.

'How was Nancy?' she asked Miles now.

'I don't know, Alexi. She was very bright and breezy, told me to stop worrying and to have a good time.' He raked a hand through thick hair. 'But, to be honest, I think she's just putting a brave face on things. I really don't think she's well. I'm just wondering if I should take a taxi and go home.'

'Take my car,' Alexandra told him firmly. She opened her handbag and dangled the keys to the Lamborghini over towards him. 'I'll get the taxi.'

He frowned. 'I can't leave you like that——'

'Of course you can.' Max interrupted their conversation smoothly. 'It will be my pleasure to take Miss Rossini home.'

A small pang of nerves started to curl inside Alexandra's stomach at that offer, but she managed to smile and nod at Miles's look of enquiry towards her.

He took the keys and leaned across to kiss her cheek. 'Thanks. I'll pick you up bright and early for work tomorrow.'

She turned her attention back to Maxwell Channing as her friend left them. 'Nancy is Miles's wife,' she told him, more for something to say to cover the feeling of awkwardness that his leaving had created within her than anything else.

'I know,' he answered easily. The blue eyes noted the way her eyebrow lifted at that. 'I asked Georgia Gold who you were with,' he explained. 'And she told me all about Miles.'

And all about me, no doubt, Alexandra thought drily. 'I see.' She sipped her champagne as she digested that piece of information. So she had been right— Maxwell had been asking Georgia about her. 'In that case you will know that Miles's car is at the garage being serviced and that I had at least six cups of black coffee at work today,' she murmured sarcastically.

'No...Georgia must be slipping. She forgot to mention you had a caffeine addiction,' Max said with a grin. 'I'll make a note to add it to the rest of the useful information she gave me.'

Alexandra would dearly have liked to ask just what exactly Georgia had told him. But she used considerable restraint, and refrained. She could guess the kind of things Georgia would have said—that she was a spoilt rich girl and that Martin Steel had broken her heart. 'It was kind of you to offer to drive me home, Mr

Channing,' she said instead. 'But I really couldn't put you to that trouble.'

'It's no trouble, I assure you, Miss Rossini.' He matched her politeness with a slightly mocking edge to his tone. 'I wouldn't have offered if it was.'

Of that Alexandra had no doubt. Maxwell Channing did not strike her as the kind of man to do anything that did not suit him.

A waiter passed by and she put down her now empty champagne glass and picked up another from the tray. She was aware that her companion's eyes never left her; they watched her every movement, and it was totally disconcerting. 'It's a lovely party, don't you think?' It was a desperate attempt at small talk as her gaze swung back to his.

The firm lips twisted in an arrogantly amused smile, and Alexandra immediately felt annoyed with herself. He knew that she was flustered. He was probably well used to having that kind of an effect on women. 'It's an interesting party.' His eyes rested on the soft curve of her lips. 'But you, on the other hand, Miss Rossini, are extremely lovely.'

Alexandra tried not to be embarrassed by the compliment. She was used to men flirting with her; she could usually handle it quite well. But this man seemed to be a master at the art of disturbing her composure. 'Thank you.' She made herself hold the direct blue eyes. 'How do you like living in California, Mr Channing?' She moved the conversation back on safer ground.

His lips curved with even more amusement. 'I think perhaps you should call me Max,' he told her lazily. 'After all, I am the man taking you home this evening.'

Alexandra hoped her face didn't look as hot as her body temperature felt at the way he said those words. He made it sound as if it were a foregone conclusion he was taking her to bed.

'As for living in California,' he continued on smoothly, 'the climate is a little more temperate than London so, in that respect, then yes, I prefer it.' He took an idle sip of his drink before continuing, 'Have you ever been to London, Alexandra?'

She noted the use of her Christian name now. She liked the way he said it; he had a beautiful voice, deep, and satin-smooth. With those looks and that voice he could have made it to the top as an actor. But Maxwell Channing was much more powerful and more successful than any Hollywood screen idol. Aware that he was waiting for her answer and that she was getting carried away with her own thoughts, she answered him quickly.

'I was sent to boarding-school over there soon after my mother died.'

He nodded, and somehow she knew that the information came as no surprise to him. Surely Georgia Gold hadn't got around to going that far back with her gossip?

'And did you like it?'

She considered that for a moment. 'It was OK, I guess, but I did feel very lonely.' She shrugged slim shoulders, feeling a little embarrassed by the admission. She had never told anyone that, so why she should give this total stranger such an intimate piece of knowledge about herself she didn't know. Maybe the champagne was going to her head.

'Well, I suppose you missed your father,' he said idly.

Alexandra glanced down at the glass in her hand. Contrary to what the media said and everyone's belief, she was not close to Henri Rossini. 'Probably,' she muttered, then glanced up at him curiously. 'Have you ever met my father?'

There was no change of expression in the flame-blue of his eyes; they burnt hard and with that strangely cold quality directly into her. 'Our paths have crossed.'

Alexandra nodded. Her father knew a lot of very in-fluential people.

Max finished his drink and placed it down on the table beside him. 'Would you like to dance, Alexandra?'

The orchestra was playing a very slow melody, the type of song that necessitated being held close. She felt a flutter of nerves as she nodded and placed her glass next to his.

She followed his broad-shouldered frame towards the dance-floor. He turned and waited for her as they reached its edge, and she smiled hesitantly up at him as his hand took hers and led her out into the midst of the dancing couples.

There was a strange moment of uncertainty as she stood opposite to him waiting for him to move closer. When he did and placed both arms around her, her heart gave a violent skip.

The sensation that flowed through her at being held by this man was electric. Every bone in her body felt charged from the warmth of his powerful frame. She had never experienced anything like it. She wondered hazily if this was what people meant when they talked about chemistry between a man and a woman. She wondered if he felt the same flow of adrenalin, the same warm, melting feeling.

She was hardly aware when the music finished; she could have gone on dancing like this all night. It was only when Max pulled away from her that she realised that the orchestra was now playing a much faster number and that most of the couples had swung into a more energetic dance.

'Shall we sit down?' he asked, a small smile playing around the corners of his mouth.

She could do no more than nod. She still felt utterly spellbound by the intensity of feeling he had just stirred up so easily.

Did he know how he was affecting her? She glanced over at him curiously as they sat down at a table by the edge of the swimming-pool.

The turquoise light from the water was reflecting on his handsome features. It was hard to read anything in the firm, rugged face. She wished that she knew more about this man; she felt totally at a loss.

'When did you meet my father?' She asked the question casually as a waiter came over towards them and they helped themselves to more drinks.

'Many years ago.' The reply was curt almost to the point of being rude.

'Pity you've missed him. He's in England filming at the moment.'

'So I understand. With your boyfriend, Martin Steel.'

He sipped at the glass of Perrier water that he had selected from the tray, and stared at her over the rim of the crystal glass.

'My ex-boyfriend,' she corrected him, and met that gaze steadily.

He smiled, but it was rather a cool smile. 'And is it true that your father disapproved of the relationship and went to great lengths to split you up?' He asked the personal question with complete ease.

Alexandra's hand tightened around the slender stem of her champagne glass. 'You would be wise not to believe everything that Georgia Gold tells you,' she said with an icy edge to her tone. The fact that there was an element of truth in this particular item of scandal galled her intensely.

'Alexandra, I always weigh the facts and draw my own conclusions,' he assured her drily. 'Do you have much contact with him now that he is away?'

'Who, my father or Martin?' she asked, somewhat perplexed by the question.

'Both, I suppose.' He took another sip of his drink and his gaze moved idly over the people around them as if he was only half interested in her answer, yet Alexandra had the distinct impression that all his senses were firmly tuned in on her.

'I haven't heard from either of them since they left last week. I probably won't until they get back.' Contrary to opinion, she wasn't overly upset about not hearing from Martin. Their relationship had not been that serious.

The conversation was ended by the arrival of Georgia Gold, who drifted over towards them, her smile firmly on Max.

'There you are, Maxwell... I hope you haven't forgotten about that dance you promised me.' Dark eyelashes fluttered and smoky grey eyes were only for him as she took the spare chair next to him.

'Georgia, you would be a hard woman to forget,' Max flirted lazily with her, and she looked extremely smug as her eyes clashed with Alexandra's across the table.

'Unfortunately I'll have to take a raincheck, as I'm just about to leave.' Max's words wiped the smile from the other woman's face, and she turned dismayed eyes on to him.

'But it's so early, darling!' The familiarity in the other woman's tone made Alexi wonder if her background had been the only topic of their earlier conversation.

Max shrugged, but attempted no explanation. 'Another time, honey.'

'I'll hold you to that,' Georgia assured him huskily. Then with a smile she rose gracefully from the table. She was wearing a silver lamé dress with a split that ran completely up one side, giving a provocative glimpse of long shapely legs. Alexi noticed that those legs did not escape Max's blue eyes.

Georgia hesitated next to Alexi. 'Did you read my column this week, Alexi?' she asked silkily.

'Sorry, Georgia, I outgrew fairy-tales a long time ago.' Alexi tempered the remark with a smile. She knew very well what Georgia had written about her, and as usual the facts had been dramatised out of all proportion.

Georgia laughed. 'I'm sorry if you didn't like it, Alexi—the truth often hurts. By the way, read it tomorrow; I'm going to do a piece about your father's little girlfriend, Monica. She's over the other side of the room having a wonderful time with our host.'

Before Alexi could say anything to that she had moved away. Alexi's mouth twisted with distaste as she looked over at Max. 'I don't know why Penny invited that woman; she's totally obnoxious.'

'Has good legs, though,' Max answered with a grin.

Alexi didn't know if she found that remark amusing. She disliked the other woman more tonight than she had ever done.

'Penny probably invited her because she wanted her party to have a mention in the papers this week,' Max continued on easily.

Alexi nodded. 'She's probably told her what to say. "Penny...looked stunning in blue. Buffet was by Harper and Jones" et cetera, et cetera.'

'Why, Alexandra, you sound less than impressed,' Max drawled in mock-horror. 'Don't you know that we are attending the best party that Hollywood has seen for...oh, at least a week?'

Alexi laughed. 'Well, if you don't mind, Max, I think your suggestion about leaving early is sounding more appealing by the moment.'

'You mean you don't mind missing the Harper and Jones experience?' he asked drolly, getting to his feet.

'I'll suffer the loss.' She stood up and glanced around for their hostess. 'Do you think we can escape without being noticed?'

'Not a chance,' Max assured her drily.

He was right; they were at least half an hour before they even reached the front door. Not only their hostess detained them, but half a dozen other people. Mostly they wanted to talk to Max.

Alexandra noticed how revered he was, how people hung on his every word, how they were quick to shower him with invitations to dinner parties and luncheons. She also noticed how skilfully he turned down the requests for his company.

They were out in the front entrance hall when Alexi literally bumped into Monica Houston. Robert James was still by her side, his arm linked with hers.

Alexi didn't much care for Monica. There was something coolly calculating about her. But her father seemed to like her and she was extremely beautiful. She looked like a Barbie doll; long blonde hair, the perfect figure and the whitest smile Alexi had ever seen. She flashed that smile at Max now as Alexi hastily introduced them.

'You must come up to the house for lunch some time, Alexi,' Monica invited smoothly now without taking her eyes from Max. 'And bring Maxwell; I'm just so lonely up there without Henri.' She turned mournful blue eyes back to Alexandra. 'You know he hasn't even bothered to phone me since he left for England.'

That didn't surprise Alexi. Her father's first love was business. His women friends seemed to come and go without causing even a ruffle to the smooth order of his life. 'Well, you know what he's like when he's working, Monica,' she said soothingly before turning her attention to Robert. 'Congratulations on your Oscar.'

'Thanks, Alexi; it's all due to your father, of course.'
He sounded as if he was making his acceptance speech
again.

Alexi smiled, congratulated him again and then Max
was steering her away and out towards the front door.

After the noise of the party the night air was blissfully
silent. Alexi followed Max to where he had parked his
car, a gleaming white Jaguar. He unlocked the doors
and they got in.

They had driven to the end of the long drive before
either of them spoke. And then it was only Max to ask
directions towards her house.

He flicked a compact disc into the player on the dash-
board, and the car was filled with the stereo sound of
Pachelbel's Canon, then Bach's *Air on the G String*.
Still neither spoke. The powerful car gobbled up the
miles.

She slanted a sideways glance at Max and then found
herself just watching him. His features were stern as he
concentrated on the road ahead, his large hands firm on
the driving-wheel. She wondered what he was thinking
about. Would he expect her to invite him in for coffee
when they got to her house... would he expect anything
else? Her nerves fluttered; if he thought that, then he
could think again. She had never been one to indulge in
casual sex.

They came up towards the gateposts of her house and
Max slowed the car and turned it skilfully into the drive.
He drove very slowly up towards the house. The outside
security lights were on and they lit up the large white
sprawling mansion.

It looked impressive now that she had had it reno-
vated. When she had first come up this driveway it had
looked sadly neglected, as if it had sat for twenty years
without anyone's love or attention. It had tugged at her
heart-strings that first day. It was a strange thing to say

you had fallen in love with a house, but she had, immediately and on first sight.

'Do you like living out here?' They were almost the first words Max had spoken since their departure, and Alexi thought his voice sounded strained; she wondered if he was tired.

'Yes, I do. I've only been living here a few months; I had an apartment downtown before that.'

'It's a little large for one, don't you think?' He cut the engine and sat looking directly out at it.

'I suppose.' She shrugged a little self-consciously. 'It was a present from my father.'

'Darling Daddy's gift.' His voice was laced with cool sarcasm. 'Georgia did warn me that you were spoilt.'

Alexi frowned, a feeling of intense hurt flooding through her. 'I don't suppose I've ever really wanted for anything materially. I wouldn't say I was spoilt, though. I work hard for the things in my life.'

'Except for your house, of course, which you gained at someone else's expense.' His tone was strangely harsh.

'It was a gift.' She shrugged; she wasn't about to start apologising for the fact that her father had money. 'You make it sound as if I've stolen it away from someone.' She turned and met his eyes directly. Hers were clear and guileless. She had nothing to be ashamed of and she was damned if she was going to allow him to treat her as if she had. 'Being wealthy isn't a crime, Max. If it was you would be in the same prison cell as my father.'

'Oh, I doubt it, Alexandra.' His voice was drily self-assured. 'I doubt that very much. Henri Rossini and I are cut from different cloths.'

Alexi felt like saying, I hope so. But she bit down on the softness of her lips. Words like that would be disloyal to her father and, although she didn't often agree with his principles in life, she was always loyal and she did love him.

'Well, thank you for the lift home.' She changed the subject and smiled at him. 'Would you like to come in for coffee?'

'Another time.' Blue eyes were sharply assessing as they met hers. 'You didn't answer my earlier question.'

'Which earlier question are you referring to?' She was parrying for time; she knew exactly what he was talking about.

'My dinner invitation, of course. Tomorrow night,' he murmured smoothly.

'You mean you still want to have dinner with me, knowing I'm Henri Rossini's rich and spoilt daughter?' Her words were spiced with amusement, but there was an element of derision aimed squarely at him.

'I knew who you were when I asked the first time,' he murmured drolly. 'But I figured, what the hell? Nobody's perfect, and you do have a near-perfect figure.' His smile was the smile of a wolf as his eyes travelled down over the curves of her body.

She fought down the colour that threatened to flood her face. 'You have a novel way of letting a woman know you are interested in her, Mr Channing.' She used his surname in a deliberate attempt to try to distance herself from his personal remarks. 'So far you have insulted me and told me that you are only interested in my body.'

He grinned, and it was the kind of wicked grin that no woman could help responding to. 'At least I'm honest, Miss Rossini. That must be a novel experience in Hollywood.'

'Probably,' she admitted with a laugh.

'So eight o'clock tomorrow evening?'

'Eight tomorrow,' she conceded. There was a moment's silence, and Alexi wondered if he was going to kiss her goodnight. Her heart thudded with increased intensity at the mere thought. He made no attempt to move anywhere near her. 'Well, goodnight, then.' She placed one hand on the door-handle.

'Until tomorrow.' He watched as she got out and climbed the two steps to her front door. Then his eyes flicked contemplatively from her over the rest of the house before he drove away, the powerful car speeding down the dark driveway.

Alexi frowned as she put her key in the lock and went inside. She wasn't sure if she was disappointed that Max hadn't kissed her, or relieved. There was something very unnerving about him. That air of raw power and sensuality that sat so easily on his broad shoulders was a powerful combination. In fact it was pretty damn lethal and it scared her to death. Dinner tomorrow suddenly loomed ahead like a trip on a giant, sensational rollercoaster.

CHAPTER THREE

'Just cast an eye over these for me, will you, Alexi?' Miles breezed into her office. He looked much more cheerful this afternoon, she thought, probably due to the fact that Nancy had called in on him at lunchtime and had looked much better.

'What are they?' She took the sheaf of papers from him and placed them over the architect's plans she had been studying.

'The accounts for the Madison kitchen. I just want you to OK them.'

Alexi smiled as she glanced down at the figures in front of her. She knew they would be right. 'These look fine, Miles. As usual you have been meticulously thorough.'

There was a brief tap on the door and her secretary came in carrying an enormous bouquet of pink and white orchids. 'These have just arrived for you, Alexi.'

Miles grinned at her. 'Martin missing you already.'

'I hardly think so. Martin is highly delighted with this part he's been given. He won't want to rock the boat with my father by sending me flowers.' There was no bitterness in Alexi's voice. She was glad for Martin, contrary to what the media and her father had thought.

She took the flowers. The sweet, delicate fragrance penetrated even the Cellophane wrapping around them. They were exquisitely beautiful. Curiously she opened the card that had accompanied them.

'Until this evening. Max.' She read the message aloud and her heart gave a crazy skip as she read the name written in the firm, flowing hand.

'Well, well. He hasn't wasted any time.' Miles sounded amused. 'You forgot to tell me how well the rest of the evening went last night.'

'There isn't much to tell; in fact we left early,' Alexi said casually as she handed the flowers back to her secretary so she could place them in water.

'Did you, now?' Miles sounded even more amused. She flashed him one of her firmly disapproving looks, and he laughed. 'Sorry, honey. But I couldn't help noticing how you looked at Channing. I have a feeling in my bones that this man is different. That you just might get serious this time.'

'Rubbish. We're just having dinner.' Alexi glanced briskly back at the work in front of her. 'And anyway, I'd say Max will only be in California temporarily on business.'

'If you say so.' Miles sounded unconvinced. 'But I do happen to know that he's bought that house out at Malibu. So he must plan to stay for a while.' Miles hesitated for a moment before continuing. 'So you had better just watch Channing, Alexi; he's one tough cookie and he does have a reputation for breaking hearts.'

'It's just dinner, Miles.' She flicked a look of irritation up at him.

'OK, OK, I just don't want to see you hurt. I'm only saying be careful.'

'I will.' She hesitated for a moment. 'Thanks, Miles.'

'For what?' He retrieved the papers that he had given her, his mind returning to business.

'For worrying about me. You and Nancy are like brother and sister to me.'

'In that case, listen to your big brother when he's advising you,' Miles said with a grin. 'Beware these men who just want to take liberties. And consider that offer on your house.' He casually tapped the letter he had left on her desk earlier. 'It's one hell of an amount and certainly worth thinking about.'

The buzz of the intercom interrupted them, and her attention was switched to taking an incoming call from one of her clients who wished to talk about the work she was having done on a bathroom.

'Yes, Mrs Patterson, gold fitments for the bathroom suite. If you will just hold on for a moment I'll get my secretary to get your file out and I'll check that for you.'

Miles mouthed goodbye to her and left her to deal with the woman.

It was some time later before Alexi put down the phone and returned to the work on her desk. She picked up the letter that Miles had been talking about and flicked through its contents for the second time that day. Whoever it was who was interested in buying her house was offering an extremely substantial amount for it, and Miles was right: the place had cost her a fortune to restore. Even now she was still feeding money into it at a rate she could barely afford, but she did love the place. For a moment practical thoughts fought with sentiment.

Her secretary came back into the room and placed the flowers that Max had sent her at the edge of her desk. 'Do me a favour, will you, Jenny?' Alexi said briskly before she could change her mind. 'Ring Morgan Real Estate and tell them I'm not interested in their client's offer for my house. That it's not for sale at any price.'

The girl nodded and left the room. Two seconds later the red light on Alexi's phone lit up and she knew the call was being placed right away. She picked up the letter, tore it neatly in half, and placed it in the litter bin. She had made the right decision, she was sure of it. This was one time when she would allow her heart to dictate to her.

Usually Alexi was ruled by her head, especially where men were concerned. Her eyes moved with a certain

scepticism over the delicate beauty of the flowers that
Maxwell Channing had sent to her. She hadn't always
been so wary; there had been a time long ago when she
had been naïvely trusting, when she had believed the
sweet endearments that men had whispered in her ears.
That childlike, trusting nature had flown out of the
window when she had been eighteen and had fallen in
love with a man whose only interest in her was the fact
that she was Henri Rossini's daughter.

Nowadays she was older and wiser and her heart was
kept under strict supervision. Sometimes that made for
a lonely existence and, for a woman who deep down had
a tender heart, she found it difficult. But it was ulti-
mately safer and much less painful. That was why she
didn't need Miles to warn her about Max. She had no
intention of lowering her guard around him. She was
intelligent enough to realise that Max had 'dangerous'
written in capital letters all over him.

Decisively she flicked the switch on her phone and
asked her secretary to come in. She was going to get on
with her work and not waste one more thought on
Maxwell Channing until this evening.

It was after six before Alexi had finished everything
and had arranged the stacks of files in their relevant order
ready to start again tomorrow. As usual she was the last
person to leave the building. She locked up behind her
and then headed for her private parking-space.

As she drove her black Lamborghini smoothly down
the busy avenues towards home her mind was still firmly
on work. But when she turned the car through her gates
and drove up the long driveway to her house it was suddenly Max that she was thinking about.

She could picture him so clearly in her mind—the
bright blue of his eyes, the dramatic darkness of his hair;
his image was sharp and clear in her memory down to
the enigmatic way he smiled at her. She tried to bring

Martin's features into her mind, but they were just a hazy blur in comparison. Strange—she had dated Martin for quite a few months and she had met Max only once.

Her house came into view, a large white building that curved in a horseshoe shape across the top of the drive. She found herself remembering the way Max had spoken about it last night. He was right, she supposed; it was far too large for just one person. It was the kind of place that cried out for a family, for weekend parties and games of tennis on the large courts that lay neglected beside it. A single girl who spent most of her time at work did not really do the place justice.

Still, she did not regret her decision to keep the house. Maybe one day she would have her own family to fill its walls with love and laughter; then it would be a real home again. The romantic notion made her lips twist wryly.

The double garage doors opened electronically for her as she drove up to them. She closed them from inside and entered the house through the internal door to the large, luxurious kitchen.

As always the heavy sound of silence was all that greeted her. She pushed a compact disc into the stereo on her way past and flicked the switches that would feed the music through the various speakers placed strategically around the house.

The moody sound of a Phil Collins song followed her out to the black wrought-iron spiral staircase and up-stairs towards the gracious splendour of her bedroom. The place was a virtual show-case for the Alexi-Miles studios. Ultra-modern and very stylish, no expense had been spared into turning the house back into the beautiful home it had once been.

She opened the double mirrored doors in her bedroom and stepped into the walk-in wardrobe. Slim fingers moved over the long rails of clothes, lingering then skipping over cashmere and silk indecisively. What should she wear tonight? What kind of a place would Maxwell Channing bring her to?

She settled for a stylish little black suit. The skirt was short and showed her long shapely legs to advantage; the lacy top was discreetly sexy. That decided, she moved back through to the bedroom and into her *en-suite* bathroom to run a shower.

She was ready well before eight o'clock and went downstairs to pour herself a glass of mineral water while she waited for Max.

She was nervous about tonight, she realised as she sat down in the sun lounge that looked out over the sprawling beauty of her gardens and down towards the curve in the driveway. She couldn't relax in the armchair and got up to walk across the deep turquoise carpets to stand for a moment by the windows.

Why on earth was she nervous? She had been out on plenty of dates with attractive men. She knew she looked good. She flicked an uncertain glance at the gilt-edged mirror beside her and relaxed. Her dark hair had a healthy shine; her wide green eyes were bright. What was the matter with her?

Miles was right when he said that Maxwell Channing was different, she acknowledged silently. He stirred up a very unusual reaction inside her. She was going to have to tread very carefully with this man. Her hands tightened around the slender stem of the crystal water glass as she noticed the dark gleam of a car pulling up her driveway.

When the doorbell rang she took her time moving towards the hall. She ran a smoothing hand over the dark gleam of her hair and, taking a deep breath, opened the front door.

It wasn't Max who stood on the doorstep, but a man in a dark chauffeur's uniform.

'Ms Rossini?' he enquired politely.

'Yes?' she murmured blankly, totally taken aback.

'Mr Channing has been delayed at a meeting today. He sends his apologies and has asked me to pick you up.'

'I see.' Her voice still held that blank tone as her mind digested this development.

'Are you ready to go, Ms Rossini?' the chauffeur asked now.

For one wild moment Alexi wanted to say no. She was in two minds about the whole invitation now. This was the kind of stunt her father played when he took out one of his many women. He too could never be bothered to break away from a business meeting, whether it was important or not. He always figured his women could wait; they slotted into a second place in his life, just as Alexi's mother had done.

Who the hell did Maxwell Channing think he was? When you asked a woman out to dinner you surely made the effort to pick her up yourself?

'Ms Rossini?' The polite tone of the chauffeur interrupted her angry thoughts. 'If you are ready?'

Alexi hesitated then shrugged. She was ready to go; it seemed childish and rather pointless to tell him otherwise. 'I'll just get my bag,' she said with quiet dignity.

The long black limousine swept slowly down the drive and out along the tranquil residential streets. Alexi paid little attention to the direction they were taking. She was still annoyed with Max. It wasn't until the limousine picked up speed and she saw the signs for Malibu beach that she sat forward to talk to her driver.

'Where exactly are we going?' she asked him, a quiver of nerves taking over from her anger.

'Mr Channing gave me instructions to take you straight to his residence.'

Alexi sat back, her anger completely forgotten now. She had thought the limousine would be taking her to some restaurant; she hadn't for one moment thought it would be taking her to his home. Warning bells were ringing somewhere deep inside her. The thought of being alone with Maxwell Channing was extremely unnerving. She took a steadying breath and told herself that she was probably only meeting him at his home, that they would go on to some restaurant.

The car pulled off the road and into the driveway of a large house that backed on to the beauty of the Pacific Ocean. Alexi's heart hammered loudly as the chauffeur climbed out and came around to open the door for her.

'Mr Channing said for you to go straight in.' The chauffeur pointed to a staircase that led up the side of the house to an upstairs door off the balcony that encircled the imposing residence.

'Thank you.' With her head held high Alexi moved gracefully up the staircase. The only sound was the gentle swish of waves against the shore and the occasional mournful cry of a seagull.

The door was ajar, and she pushed it and walked straight in.

The house was like a film set. Polished wooden floors gave the illusion of being on a ship's deck. Brass gleamed against the dark panels of the wall and the ocean beckoned through the long glass doors that completely covered the end of the room.

A table was set for two beside those doors. Candlelight flickered on the intimate table set with polished silver and a centre-piece of three red roses. Through the glass doors the sun was setting in a glorious ball of red fire into the ocean. The scene was so blatantly romantic that Alex felt her heart start up a rapid and very apprehensive tattoo.

'Ah, Ms Rossini.' A woman stepped from the shadows of the room and smiled at her. 'I am Rosie, Mr Channing's housekeeper. Mr Channing won't be long. Can I take your jacket?'

Alexi allowed the older woman to take the black cashmere jacket from her, and she was shown to a settee which sat back from a bar area.

'I've taken the liberty of mixing you a Martini cocktail. I hope that meets with your approval?' The woman went behind the bar and smiled over at her.

'That would be lovely, thank you,' Alexi said, her eyebrows lifting a little in surprise. Martini was her favourite aperitif.

The woman poured her drink and placed it on the table next to her then disappeared. There was no background music in the room; the only sound was the muted rumble of the ocean which seemed to permeate the room as if it were a ship alone at sea.

She sipped her drink and her eyes wandered to the view of the sea and then lingered on the table set for two. Obviously they were dining here, alone. For a moment her mind ran back to that ridiculous conversation they had had at the Jameses' party. What had Max said? First dinner, followed by a late breakfast... Her pulses quickened nervously. If he thought he was going to get her into bed so easily, he could think again.

'Ah, Alexandra. My apologies for running a little behind schedule.' Max came into the room, his deep voice booming into the silence and startling her.

She turned her head and their eyes met.

He looked magnificent; there was no other adjective to describe him. The dark suit sat so well on his powerful frame. His features, so rugged and arrogantly tough, made her heart jump.

His dark eyes moved over her, like a panther weighing up its prey. They took in the long shapely legs in the black mini skirt, the curve of her breast under the black lace and the long shining length of her hair.

'May I say you look extremely beautiful.' The compliment was given very smoothly. He was well practised in the art of wooing a woman; Alexi had no doubt about that.

'Thank you.' She tried very hard not to be flattered.

'I thought we would dine here.' Max moved with lithe grace behind the bar and helped himself to a measure of bourbon from one of the optics. 'I hope that meets with your approval? I thought it would be a more relaxed setting for us to get to know one another, and Rosie really is an excellent cook.'

Alexi didn't feel in the slightest bit relaxed—in fact she felt at a distinct disadvantage—but she nodded and took a sip of her Martini. It was strong, but the fiery liquid gave a soothing feeling to the rumble of apprehension. 'Thank you for the flowers, by the way. They were beautiful,' she murmured.

He inclined his head in acknowledgement, then carried his drink over towards her and, instead of sitting in the chair opposite, he sat next to her on the couch.

'So, Alexandra.' He angled himself around so that he could look into her eyes. 'What do you think of my L.A. abode?'

'It's very...dramatic.' Alexi glanced around again, trying not to notice how close he was sitting to her, and the subtle tang of his cologne that made her want to close her eyes and breathe in deeply.

'Yes...it is. Later I'll show you around; there are one or two rooms I'd like you to change for me. The bedroom, for instance, could do with your expert attention.' There was a sardonically amused note to the velvet-deep voice.

Alexi took a deep drink of her Martini before meeting his eyes directly. 'As long as you don't intend asking me to stay for breakfast, I would be pleased to look over the room.'

The firm mouth slanted in an arrogant smile. 'Why, Alexandra, what a devious mind you credit me with.' His blue eyes held a mocking glint. 'When I want you to stay for breakfast I will ask you openly and directly.'

His words were arrogant, as if he was certain that she was his for the asking. Had no woman ever refused him? Alexi found herself wondering with irritation.

'I think we had already decided to skip the breakfast, marriage and divorce and stick to the realistic work,' she reminded him crisply.

'Imagine remembering that.' He shook his head in mock-horror. 'I would never have taken you for such a spoil-sport.'

'I don't look on sex as sport.' Alexi took another sip of her drink. 'So as long as you're not regarding me as fair game we will get along together fine.'

'Then I can see trouble brewing, because I definitely regard you as fair game.' He gave her a rakish grin that made her unsure if he was joking or not.

'Should I serve dinner now, Mr Channing?' Rosie enquired from the doorway.

'Thank you, Rosie.' Max stood up and Alexi followed him. She was relieved that their conversation had been interrupted; it had definitely been heading off at a strange tangent. How was it that Max always managed to make her feel at a disadvantage?

He held a chair for her as she sat down, then sat opposite. His manners were smoothly correct at all times, Alexi noticed. She watched him discreetly as their first course of salmon mousse was served.

He thanked the housekeeper as she retreated back towards the kitchen and then reached to fill Alexi's crystal goblet with white wine.

His skin was lightly tanned from the Californian sun; it contrasted crisply with the stark white of his silk shirt, probably bought from some expensive boutique on Rodeo Drive. His hands looked strong and powerful beside the slender stem of his wine goblet.

She met his gaze across the table and felt her skin grow hot as he caught her watching him. She reached for her wine glass and took a sip to cover the awkward moment. The wine was cool and crisp and very familiar. Her eyes moved to the table and noted it was her favourite white wine.

'Do you like working as an interior design artist, Alexandra?'

She smiled and relaxed immediately at this topic of conversation. 'The Alexi-Miles studio is the main love of my life,' she answered him truthfully. Her love for her work had filled a void in her life, an emptiness that had been there for a long time.

'The studio is in a very elite part of town; the overheads must be colossal.'

She nodded. 'But we need to be there in order to attract the right clientele. Luckily we are kept very busy.' She crossed slender fingers and smiled at him.

His eyes rested for a brief moment on the soft curve of her mouth, and there was a strange expression in the bright blue eyes. It wasn't the lascivious look that some men gave when they wanted to get her into their bed. Alexi couldn't fathom it at all; it was more a look of indecision, a look that said he wasn't quite certain of something, and that was intensely puzzling because she knew without a doubt that Maxwell Channing was not a man who suffered from indecision ... and anyway, indecision about what?

'I suppose your father financed the business,' he remarked lazily.

'Then you suppose wrong.' She glared at him. He really did think she was some kind of spoilt little rich girl who had never stood on her own two feet. Her father had offered to finance them, but she had firmly refused the offer. She hadn't wanted to be in any way indebted to Henri Rossini; she knew her father well enough to know that the only reason he had offered was the fact that he liked to dictate terms, he liked to have power over her, just as he liked to wield power over everything else in his life.

'Miles and I lease the building. We are up to here in debt.' She held a delicate hand up to her forehead. 'But the only people we are in debt to is the bank; we've done everything on our own. We're just worried at the moment that our rent is going to be increased dramatically; if so we might just have to move from there, and I think such a move could be very damaging for the business.' At the same time as she was talking she was wondering why on earth she was telling him all this. It was very unlike her to reveal such private things. 'But I'm sure we'll work it all out,' she finished suddenly with embarrassment.

'With a little help from Daddy's contacts?' The velvet-deep voice sounded amused.

Green eyes glimmered with annoyance. 'And I suppose you have never used a contact in your life?' she asked with barely veiled sarcasm.

'I'm not saying anything of the kind,' he replied easily. 'I just find you surprising, that's all.'

'Surprising?' She frowned at this statement.

'You've been brought up surrounded by wealth and riches and yet you have a fiercely independent streak. I find that very surprising.' He reached over and topped up her wine glass. 'Every time I mention that you might have had a helping hand in life, you burn with rage.'

'That might have something to do with the fact that you make me sound like a spoilt brat.'

'Do I?' He sounded unconcerned.

'Yes, you do.' She twirled the crystal goblet idly between slender fingers. 'And it might interest you to know that I wasn't always brought up surrounded by riches. My parents were divorced when I was just a baby. I lived with my mother in a modest house and I had no contact with my father until she died.'

'How old were you then?' Max finished his first course and sat back to watch her with interest.

'Twelve.'

'It must have been hard for you.' There was a note of sympathy in the deep tone.

She nodded. She couldn't bring herself to tell him just how hard it had been. Her mother had been a warm, loving person. Losing her and moving to live with her father had been a traumatic experience.

Henri Rossini had had no time for a twelve-year-old girl. He had been coldly remote and very strict. On her thirteenth birthday she had been sent away to boarding-school in England.

'Still, you have never wanted for anything,' he went on briskly. 'Henri Rossini has pampered your every whim.'

Her lips curved in a bittersweet smile. That certainly wasn't true. She couldn't blame Max for thinking that way; the media had certainly gone to town on giving her that kind of image. Maybe materially speaking it was true; she had attended the best schools and colleges and she had never been short of money. But money wasn't everything. Emotionally, Henri Rossini had neglected her completely; she had received no affection, no love in her upbringing with him.

She didn't correct his assumption and she avoided meeting his gaze. She had no wish for him to see the bleakness in her eyes. 'You're right; I had everything money could buy,' she said brightly, perhaps a little too brightly.

The housekeeper returned with their main course at that moment, much to Alexi's relief. She had no wish to talk on this subject any longer. Strange how just thinking back to her childhood could still upset her so much.

Rosie cleared away the other dishes and retired quietly.

'Beef *flamande*, one of my favourite dishes,' Alexi remarked as she looked down at the beautifully presented meal.

'I'm glad you approve. Rosie is an excellent cook,' he said easily.

'She is also remarkably adept at choosing my favourite food and drink. So far she has got everything right from the aperitif to her choice of vegetables.'

'As I said, she is a remarkable woman,' Max said with a grin.

'A treasure,' she murmured, a puzzled frown marring her smooth forehead. Was it just coincidence that all her favourite things had been placed before her? Or had Max deliberately done some homework on her to discover her personal preferences?

'I have a file on you this big,' Max said, correctly reading what was running through her mind and holding his hands up to indicate a file of enormous proportions.

Their eyes met across the candlelight and she laughed. Of course it was a coincidence; a busy man like Maxwell Channing wouldn't be interested in the small details of her likes and dislikes. The idea was ludicrous.

Her laughter dispelled the shadows that had been hanging over her, and she smiled over at him. He smiled back. He had a very attractive smile, but it didn't quite reach the blue of his eyes. Sometimes he looked at her so oddly, she thought idly. Almost as if he was assessing her in a very detached, calculating way.

'You have a beautiful smile, Alexandra,' he said in a smooth, deep tone. 'It's bright and vivacious and sometimes strangely vulnerable.'

'Well, thank you for the compliment.' She inclined her head stiffly, feeling a little disconcerted by his observations. Obviously she hadn't been far wrong when she had imagined him studying her closely. 'But I wouldn't class myself as vulnerable.'

'No?' One dark eyebrow lifted.

'No. I know exactly how to take care of myself. I'm a good business person and I survive very nicely in the cut-and-thrust world of Beverly Hills. I'd hardly think that makes for a vulnerable person.' Her voice was crisply cool, her young face unconsciously militant. Alexandra didn't like anyone to think she was in any way vulnerable. She had worked very hard at cultivating a confident and at times tough exterior. She didn't want anyone to penetrate behind that mask, least of all Maxwell Channing.

'So there is a little bit of your father's blood racing around in that beautiful body after all?' he drawled softly. 'An ambitious, rather ruthless temperament hiding behind those large green eyes.'

She couldn't tell if he was mocking her now. Looking at the twist of his arrogant mouth, she assumed that he was.

'But of course,' she agreed with him in a lightly flippant tone. 'So you see, you cross a Rossini at your own peril.' She was joking, but suddenly he looked intently serious.

He paused with his hand on the crystal goblet he had been about to raise to his lips. 'I'm glad you have told me that, Alexandra. It makes being with you that much easier.' There was a strangely chilling edge to his voice.

She frowned as she stared over at him. 'I'm sorry, I don't understand...'

'I mean, my dear Alexandra, that I like to have a worthy opponent sitting across the table from me. It means I can pursue you with no holds barred. I'd much rather chase after the beautiful, sly fox than the small, timorous gazelle.' The dry amusement was back in his tone now.

'And are you pursuing me?' She met that cool blue-eyed look head-on.

'But of course. And I think it's going to be an extremely profitable exercise,' he said smoothly.

Her eyes widened slightly. 'I beg your pardon?'

He smiled easily. 'You're a highly desirable woman, Alexandra. Well worth the chase.'

Alexi wasn't sure how she should reply to that. She presumed when he spoke about chasing her he meant into his bed. She had never met any man who was quite so direct about his intentions; it was very unnerving. 'I may as well tell you that I don't approve of blood sports,' she murmured uneasily.

He smiled. 'Approve or not, the hounds have tasted your scent and are on the trail.' He lifted his glass in a sardonic salute. 'To a worthy opponent.'

'There is a phone call for you, Mr Channing.' The housekeeper's voice interrupted them from the doorway. 'Would you like to take it in here?'

'Who is it, Rosie?' There was a hint of impatience in Max's tone, giving Alexi the impression that he had told the woman he didn't want to be disturbed.

'It's your attorney. He did say it was important.'

'OK, Rosie. I'll take it in the study.' Max rose to his feet. 'Excuse me, Alexandra; I won't be a moment.'

He was gone for quite some time. Alexi had finished her main course and Rosie was clearing away the dishes from the table when he returned.

'Sorry about that.' He sat back down and indicated to the housekeeper that she could take his plate too. 'A little bit of business that wouldn't wait, I'm afraid.'

'That's OK.' She met his eyes across the candlelit table. 'What kind of business are you out here on, Max?' She asked the question that she had been wondering about as she'd sat waiting for him.

'The unfinished kind.' He grinned. 'Really I should be over in New York at the moment. But unfortunately I have some loose ends to tie up here, and they require my personal attention.'

'I see.' She finished the last of her wine and sat back in her chair. 'You remind me of my father. He spends most of his time dashing around the world on urgent business. Sometimes he could do with being in two countries at the same time.'

'Yes. The film industry does keep you constantly on your toes,' Max agreed drily.

'Do you enjoy the work?'

'The Brightwell studios are something of a hobby; I look in on it occasionally, but I'm constantly on the look-out for new challenges—I always enjoy a challenge.' He met her eyes with that direct look she was learning to expect from him. 'How about a stroll along the beach before we have our dessert?' His voice was warmly intimate now and it stirred something to life inside her.

This man was too damned attractive, she thought as she nodded her acquiescence and got to her feet. The mere hint of warmth in his tone seemed to light some kind of answering flame within her. It was most disconcerting.

They stepped out through the sliding glass doors on to the balcony. The night air was a little cool, and Max immediately asked her if she would like her jacket.

She shook her head. 'No, I'll be all right once we start walking.'

They moved to the steps that led down to the shore, and Max put a guiding arm under her elbow. His mere touch sent a shiver of awareness racing through her. What was it about this man that made all her senses seem so sharply tuned in?

She left her shoes at the bottom of the steps and they walked out across the soft sand. Moonlight reflected in the dark sea like a sprinkle of silver coins. The breeze whipped Alexi's long hair and left a salty tang against the softness of her lips.

'Beautiful out here, isn't it?' Max spoke absently, almost to himself. 'I love the wild, unleashed power of the ocean.'

She glanced up at him, startled by the observation. For a moment he didn't seem to notice that all her attention was tuned into him. He stared out over the sea, lost in his own private thoughts. The rugged features were cast into shadow by the moonlight. They looked bleak for a second, and there was an almost cruel twist to the sensual lips.

She shivered involuntarily and he glanced down at her. 'Cold?'

Before she could answer he had reached out an arm and placed it around her shoulders, pulling her closely in against him.

She was acutely aware of the penetrating warmth of his body heat as they walked on in silence. She couldn't remember being this conscious of any man before. He made her heart race and her mouth feel dry; he made her want to snuggle in even closer. It was a ludicrous feeling. She hardly knew Maxwell Channing; how could the sensations he stirred up be so intense?

'Whereabouts do you live in England, Max?' Suddenly she was filled with a consuming need to know more about him.

'I have a house on the banks of the River Thames in London.'

'Do you live alone?'

He stopped walking and turned towards her with a smile. 'Is that your roundabout way of asking if there are any women in my life?'

'No.' She was glad of the darkness, because her cheeks were burning with hot colour. 'I'm just curious about your life in England.'

'Well, I have a good life. I work hard and I play hard,' he said with some amusement in his tone. 'And I live alone.'

'Oh.' She didn't know what else to say. He had succeeded in making her feel very foolish, something he seemed very adept at.

He tipped her chin so that she was forced to meet his gaze. 'Happy?' he murmured in a husky undertone.

She shrugged. 'It's nothing to me who you live with,' she said defensively.

'No?' Again there was that arrogantly amused tone to his voice. His hand moved and his thumb stroked at the soft, vulnerable curve of her lower lip. The sensation made her tremble.

For a wild moment she wanted him to kiss her; she really thought that he was going to kiss her. He was so close. Her heart went into overdrive and her dark lashes closed over her eyes, inviting his caress.

'I think we should go back inside. You're shivering.'

His crisp tone made her eyes fly open. There was a glimmer of confusion in them as she stared up at him. 'If you want.' Desperately she strove to rid her voice of the raw edge of hurt. Why hadn't he kissed her? Had she read the signals wrong? She tried to tell herself that it really didn't matter to her. But deep down it did matter, and she felt stung with a strange feeling of rejection.

The house was warm after the cool night air. There was a delicious aroma of freshly brewed coffee, and a log fire now blazed brightly in the stone fireplace.

Rosie heard them come in and she came to ask what they would like for dessert. 'I have raspberry pavlova or you can have chocolate brandy-snaps with fresh cream,' she said brightly.

'Just coffee for me, please,' Alexi told her as she sat back down on the settee.

'Not on a diet, I hope?' Max enquired lazily as he went behind the bar and poured them both a brandy.

'No, but I couldn't possibly manage anything more. The meal was delicious.'

'I'm glad you enjoyed it.' He came and handed her the drink. His hand brushed against hers lightly as she took the glass. It was just an accident, something that with any other man wouldn't have caused her a moment's thought. The slight contact made her pulse-rate quicken. 'I've enjoyed your company very much.' He stood next to her and she had to tip her head right back in order to see him properly. 'What do you say we do it again...Saturday night? I'll take you to a nice little seafood restaurant I know.'

'That would be nice, Max.' There was a genuine note of pleasure in her voice. She had wondered when he hadn't kissed her if maybe he wouldn't want to see her again. If maybe he wasn't really attracted to her. Strange how the thought of never seeing him again had been so dismaying.

'How long do you think you will be in L.A. for?' she asked casually now.

'For as long as my business takes.' He shrugged broad shoulders and sat down next to her. 'I intend to keep this house as a base for at least a couple of years, but whether I actually get to spend much time here is another matter.'

'I see.' She glanced down at the brandy glass. Maxwell Channing was probably just passing through; she would do well to remember that and the fact that in all likelihood he probably had a dozen dates lined up for his time in California.

She looked up at him and he smiled, then stretched out one hand to trail a finger delicately down the side of her cheekbone. The feeling sent a delicious shiver racing down her spine. 'I think maybe that my business here might take a little longer than I expected,' he murmured.

'Might it?' Her voice sounded breathless, even to her own ears. Her heart thumped uneasily as he moved to put down his glass on the table beside them.

The sensual lips curved in an arrogant smile. 'Oh, yes,' he assured her, a roguish glint in those deep blue eyes. 'I can see a number of complications settling in already.'

She caught her breath as he came closer towards her. His hand moved up to trail softly through the silky texture of her long hair. Then his head lowered and his lips met hers.

At first his kiss was light against the soft curve of her mouth. She could taste the faint trace of brandy against the warmth of his lips. The sensation was heady and she responded gently, her heart pounding. Then the kiss deepened and all her senses heightened as she leaned against him and gave herself up to the exquisite pleasure of being in his arms. She had never experienced such a kiss. It made her blood sing in her veins; it made her forget all caution. All she could remember was the desire to love and be loved in return.

He pulled away from her and for a moment they just stared into each other's eyes. The silence between them was only broken by the soft crackle of the fire; it seemed to match the flame of desire that had raged through Alexi's body. She gazed up at him, a light of stunned amazement in her eyes. She couldn't remember any man ever arousing her so completely, so quickly.

'Are you working in the morning?' His voice held a husky rasp. She had the feeling that he felt as startled as she did by the intensity of passion that had flared so suddenly between them. His eyes were a deep, deep, all-consuming blue. He was certainly not unaffected by her.

'Yes.' She swallowed hard and forced herself to move completely away from him.

'You could stay here. I'll get Steve to run you in in the morning.'

It was a casually voiced request. Max moved to pick up his coffee-cup, and suddenly reality started to set in.

As much as she might be tempted to stay with him, she knew she couldn't. One-night stands were not for her. She couldn't stay, then leave calmly tomorrow as if nothing had happened. 'I can't, Max,' she murmured in a shaky tone. She didn't sound as urbanely cool as he had when he had asked her to stay, she thought dismally.

'That's OK, Alexandra,' he said smoothly. 'Another time.'

She angled a look across at him. He was once more in complete control of the situation. Had she imagined when he had kissed her that he had nearly lost that cool command that always seemed to surround him? The idea seemed almost ludicrous now.

She got stiffly to her feet and brushed a smoothing hand down imaginary creases in the short black skirt. His eyes followed the nervous movement of her hand, then lingered on the slender length of her legs before moving slowly and seductively over the gentle curve of her hips and waist and then on to her breasts. The gaze seemed so intent on taking in every detail of her figure that she could almost feel his eyes like a caress against her skin.

Heat seared her face. 'I...I have to go, Max,' she mumbled now, and he smiled as he rose with agile grace to stand beside her.

'Of course.' Without any further preamble he moved out of the room to get her jacket.

'I hope you don't mind, but I asked Steve to take you home,' he said when he returned.

'No...no, that's fine.' A part of her was relieved; if he had kissed her again outside her house she might have been tempted to ask him in. On the other hand there was a little part of her that resented that offhand attitude of his.

He helped her into her jacket and his hand lingered for a fraction of a second on her shoulder as he walked with her towards the door.

They walked out into the cool night air and, looking down the steps to the front of the house, she noted that his chauffeur was already standing next to the limousine waiting for her.

'It's all right, Max, you don't need to come down with me,' she told him as he made to walk down the steps beside her.

'Of course I do. It's the least I can do to see you safely into the car.' His hand was tucked firmly under her arm as he walked beside her. She wished with all her heart that she weren't so acutely conscious of it.

The chauffeur opened the rear door as they reached the bottom of the steps. They walked over and stood next to it. Alexandra's heart was hammering painfully as she turned to say goodbye to him.

'Thank you for a lovely meal.' She stared up into the deep midnight colour of his eyes.

'Thank you.'

She couldn't help thinking how incredibly polite it all was, the calm restraint in no way matching the explosion that had been created by one kiss. Would he kiss her goodnight?

A faint smile softened the arrogant curve of his mouth. 'Goodnight, Alexandra.' His lips touched hers in a feather-light caress that was over almost before it had begun, leaving the cool night air to wash over her as he moved away. 'Until next time.'

CHAPTER FOUR

ALEXI was painting a windowsill at the front of her house. It was Saturday afternoon, and for once she had finished work early enough to get through a few odd jobs at home that there hadn't been time for lately. It was a hot day and she was wearing shorts and a T-shirt, her long dark hair drawn back into a ponytail.

She heard the engine of a car as it turned up her drive, and grimaced. Added to the fact that she wasn't dressed to receive visitors, she was in no mood for them. In fact she had been very on edge for a couple of days now, ever since her date with Maxwell Channing.

She had expected him to ring to confirm their date tonight, but he hadn't. She could only assume that because she had refused his invitation to stay the night he had lost interest in her. That angered her on two counts: firstly that he should turn out to be that kind of a man, and secondly that she should give a damn.

She heard a car door slamming and put down her paint-brush to turn and see who her visitor was.

'Ms Rossini?' The man standing next to the shiny red sports car was a stranger to her.

'Yes.' She wiped her hands on the cloth next to her and went to see what he wanted.

He was about her own age and quite attractive. 'I'm John Yates, of Morgan Real Estate.'

Alexi's lips tightened. 'I see.'

'I wondered if I might have a word with you, Ms Rossini?'

Alexi took a deep breath. 'If it's about the offer on my house then I'd rather not waste your time, Mr Yates. My house is not for sale. I thought I'd made that perfectly clear.'

'Yes, you did,' the man said calmly. 'But I have been instructed to offer you a higher price and I thought you might like to talk it over.'

'No, I do not wish to talk it over.' Alexi shook her head very definitely.

'Perhaps when you hear the amount we have been authorised to offer.' The man then went on to name a sum that for a moment made Alexi just gaze at him in astonishment.

Then she laughed; the amount was so high that it was quite preposterous. 'May I ask who it is that has placed the offer?'

'I'm sorry, Ms Rossini, I am not at liberty to say,' the man replied calmly.

'Well, I don't know what your client is playing at, but my house is not for sale, at any price. Perhaps you would tell him that?'

A brief look of irritation flashed over the smooth features. 'I urge you very strongly to consider the offer, Ms Rossini. It is an extortionately generous one, well over the property's market value.'

'I'm aware of that, Mr Yates,' Alexi retorted crisply. 'What I don't understand is your client's motives. Why is he so eager to buy a house that isn't for sale?'

The man shrugged. 'Does it matter? Surely the important issue is the money being offered.'

'The important issue is the house is not for sale,' Alexi reiterated. 'Now good day to you.'

The man was clearly annoyed now, but he turned and without any further words got back into his car.

Alexi picked up her paintbrush and went back inside the house to wash it off. Who on earth could want her house so badly that they would offer that kind of money? Alex wondered as she stood at the kitchen sink. It was very irritating and intensely mysterious.

There was a ring at the front door and Alexi sighed in frustration. If that was Mr Yates back again she would be furious.

She could see the gleam of red through the misty glass panels of her front door, and her lips tightened angrily. 'Look, Mr Yates, I've told you I'm not interested...' Her voice trailed off in horror as she saw that it was not the agent who stood outside but Max Channing. 'Max!' She stared at him, horrified that he should find her in this dishevelled state.

His eyes moved with lazy amusement over her slender figure in the brief shorts and cropped top. 'You look about sixteen,' he observed drily, his eyes moving to the ponytail and her face, naked of any make-up. 'Where is the sophisticated Alexandra Rossini who I dined with the other night?'

'She's having the afternoon off to paint the windowsills,' Alexi informed him with a rueful smile. 'If she had known you were coming she would have dressed accordingly.'

'In that case I'm glad I didn't tell her. I think I prefer her just like that,' he said smoothly.

She smiled and shook her head at such a flippant remark. 'Compliments will get you everywhere,' she told him with a laugh as she stepped back to allow him inside.

'I should be so lucky.' He stepped past her. 'And who is Mr Yates and what have you told him you're not interested in?'

'He's from Morgan Real Estate. Making an offer on behalf of someone who wants to buy my house.' She led the way through to the kitchen.

'I didn't know you were selling your house.' He sat down at the kitchen table as she filled the kettle for some coffee.

'I'm not. That's the strange thing. I've had three offers now from some mysterious person who doesn't even want to give his name.'

'And were the offers good?' Max enquired lazily.

'Yes, they were.' Alexi put some cream and some cups and saucers on the table then sat down. 'In fact the last one was extremely good.'

'And are you tempted?' Max asked casually.

'No,' Alexi said firmly. 'I like living here.'

'Everyone has a price, Alexandra,' he drawled, a hint of amusement in his deep tone. 'I think give it a little time and your mystery man will find yours.'

'I don't agree,' Alexi said with firm conviction. 'Not everyone can be bought. I certainly can't.' She got up to pour the boiling water into the coffee-pot.

'No?' He shrugged broad shoulders. 'Well, I suppose only time will answer that.' He leaned back in his chair, an attractive half-smile tugging at the corners of his mouth. 'In the meantime, how about dinner tonight? I did book a table for seven o'clock.'

'You did?' She glanced over at him in surprise.

'Well, don't look so amazed. I did ask you if you were free tonight. I thought you said yes.'

'I did. I just thought...' She stumbled to a halt, not really wanting to tell him what she had thought. It was not particularly flattering that she had presumed he had lost interest because she wouldn't go to bed with him. 'When you didn't ring I just assumed you had forgotten about me or some important business had cropped up.'

He smiled. 'You are my important business, Alexandra. I was going to suggest that if you've finished work we could go out now, make a day of it.'

It was still early, just after one, and she did have a host of other jobs waiting. But it was a lovely day and just looking at Max relaxing at her kitchen table, so incredibly handsome in light-coloured chinos and a shirt a few shades lighter than the deep blue of his eyes, made her feel unexplainably light-hearted and frivolous.

'Well, what about it?' he prompted her, a teasing light in those gorgeous eyes.

'It sounds wonderful. I'll just run upstairs and change while you drink your coffee.' She placed the pot on the table in front of him.

His eyes moved over the bare length of her legs. 'You don't have to for me,' he assured her lazily. 'You look perfect the way you are.' Taking her unawares, he caught her arm and she unbalanced easily down on to his lap. 'Absolutely perfect,' he reiterated in a husky tone before his lips captured hers in a strong and fleeting caress that was over almost before it had started.

'But if you must be a spoil-sport and cover those lovely legs I suppose you'd better hop to it.' He released her so that she could stand up again. Which she did on legs that felt decidedly unsteady.

'I won't be long,' she told him, her voice wavering slightly.

He grinned and reached for the coffee as she hurriedly left him.

She had to sit down on her bed when she reached her room. It was crazy; one little flirtatious incident, one little kiss, and she had completely gone to pieces, like a schoolgirl with an almighty crush. It was completely unnerving.

She glanced over and caught her reflection in the mirror. 'You'll have to tread very carefully here, Alexi,' she told herself softly. Dating this man could seriously damage that tough outer shell that she liked to keep around her heart. 'He'll be going back to England soon,' she reminded herself briskly. 'So there is no point in becoming too attracted to him.'

She took the tie from her hair and shook it free, then leaned across to get the hairbrush from her bedside cabinet. Her eyes fell on the framed photograph of her parents that always sat next to her bed, and her lips curved in a sad smile.

It had been taken on their wedding-day. Alexi's mother was looking up at her husband with adoring eyes. Henri Rossini was looking directly at the camera, a look of pride on his handsome features. The photograph had always sat next to her mother's bed. Even though they had been divorced her mother had never stopped loving him.

'He's not a bad man, Alexi,' she had told her daughter shortly before she had died. 'I know in his own way he still loves me very much. It's just that he couldn't love me enough.'

For a moment Alexi closed her eyes, remembering those words with the same pangs of utter sadness she had felt back then when they had been spoken.

'He didn't love me enough to overcome that stubborn pride of his and admit he was wrong. He didn't love me enough to make time for me out of that busy schedule of his. It was that that tore our marriage apart. No other man, no other woman. Love is like a flower, Alexi. If it's not looked after and nourished, it fades away and dies.'

Alexi brushed a hand over the wetness of her cheek. Why on earth was she sitting here feeling so upset about something so distantly in the past? She got up from her bed and opened the wardrobe to search for something to wear. Bearing in mind that Max was casually dressed, she selected a pair of designer jeans and a white gypsy-style top that could be worn off the shoulders. Then she headed for the shower.

She was back downstairs twenty minutes later.

'I'm in here, Alexandra,' Max's voice called to her as she reached the bottom of the stairs, and she went through to the sun lounge.

He was standing next to the windows, looking out towards the sweeping lawns. 'The house has a beautiful secluded outlook,' he remarked idly as he turned.

'Yes, there is nothing behind here; it's completely private.' She crossed to stand next to him. 'My father bought it originally because he was interested in buying the land behind it and developing the whole lot into some kind of leisure complex. Unfortunately...' she paused and then grinned '... or fortunately, as the case may be for me, someone else bought the land before he did. It spoilt all his plans and I ended up getting the house. Lucky for some, don't you think?'

'I guess so.' Max smiled; it was a cool smile. 'If you are ready I think we should go; time is moving on.'

Max was driving a red convertible Mercedes.

'Where's the Jaguar you were driving last week?' Alexi asked as she settled herself in the passenger seat.

'For me, variety is the spice of life. I like change, stops me from getting bored.' He flashed her a white grin. 'Some men like to change wives every other week; with me it's cars.'

'Well, you don't have a wife to change,' Alexi retorted with a shake of her head.

'That is true.' He put his foot down on the accelerator and they took off at speed down her drive. The breeze caught Alexi's hair and whipped it around her face in glossy disorder. She pushed it back with an impatient hand.

'Why is that?' she asked curiously. 'How have you managed to escape to the ripe old age of...what? Thirty-five? Without some woman catching you?'

He smiled. 'That's a very leading question. Why is it women are always insatiably curious about such things?'

She considered the question for a moment. 'Probably because the answer will give a woman an immediate insight into your character.'

'I see.' He pursed his lips and thought for a moment. 'Well, the reason I'm not married, Alexandra, is that I enjoy my freedom. I'm a busy man with no time for serious ties, and besides, as I said before, I consider variety to be the spice of life.' He glanced over at her. 'Have I given you an immediate insight into my character?' he asked drolly.

She nodded. 'It's just as I suspected,' she replied in a quietly humorous tone. 'You are an out and out wolf.'

He laughed at that. 'You're probably right, Alexandra. A man to be avoided at all costs.'

His laughter was warm and incredibly attractive. It made a tingle race through Alexi's body.

'Which of course is why women find you irresistible,' she replied, trying to ignore the sensations racing through her.

'Is that what it is?' He turned blue eyes on her, a wicked glint in their sapphire depths. 'So what about you, Alexandra? Why are you not married?'

'Maybe, like you, I enjoy my freedom too much,' she said flippantly.

'I can see we're a match made in heaven.' He caught hold of her hand and raised it to his lips. The softness of his lips against the palm of her hand made her shiver. She pulled it away abruptly from him. She didn't like the way he was able to create such havoc with her senses; it made her very nervous.

'So where are we going?' she asked brightly, trying to bring the conversation around to safer ground.

'To a good little seafood restaurant I know.'

She nodded. 'Where?'

'San Francisco,' he replied levelly.

'San Francisco!' She swivelled around in her seat. 'That's miles away.'

'Which is why we're heading for the airport. I have a private jet standing by.'

'Of course.' Alexi turned her attention to the passing scenery. 'If you're anything like my father you'll have your plane on permanent stand-by,' she remarked idly. When she had lived at home she had hardly seen anything of her father.

'Well, as you know, I do a lot of travelling. The plane is convenient.'

The plane turned out to be a magnificent Lear jet. 'I don't know about convenient,' Alexi said as she looked around the interior. 'It's extremely luxurious.'

'It's adequate.' Max waved her towards one of the comfortable chairs. 'Let's get ready for take-off, shall we? Then I'll show you around.'

She sat down beside him and fastened her seatbelt. A screen rolled down in front of them as Max flicked a button on the arm of his chair. It showed a map of where they were and the flight path they would be taking to San Francisco. As the plane moved down the runway, it showed the speed they were doing and the temperature outside. The relaxing music of the Righteous Brothers filtered through the plane as it built up speed and swept easily up and away from the ground.

The seatbelt sign flicked off and Max stood up. 'Come on, I'll show you my little home away from home.'

Alexi followed him through the room they were in, which was skilfully decorated to look like a lounge. Next to it was a small study with a desk. Then a galley kitchen, which Max walked into.

'We'll have a drink while we're here,' he said, opening the fridge and taking out a bottle of champagne. He opened it easily and poured out two glasses into delicate crystal flutes.

'To a successful liaison.' He raised his glass towards hers and took a sip.

'I don't know if I like the sound of that.' She angled her chin upwards to look at him. 'It suggests something illicit.'

'Does it?' He shrugged broad shoulders. 'Well, it sounds a little more exciting than just drinking to a pleasant day out.'

She thought about that for a moment. 'Well, let's drink to our friendship, then.' She raised her glass and tasted the sparkling liquid.

He didn't join her in the toast; instead he turned to leave the kitchen, picking up the champagne bottle as he went. 'Come on, I'll show you the last room,' he said easily.

The room next door turned out to be a bedroom. Extremely luxurious, very masculine.

'Maybe we can drink to our friendship in here one day.' He grinned as he noticed the flood of colour to her cheeks as she took in the double bed.

'Why, Alexandra, you look disconcerted,' he said in a teasing tone.

'Not at all.' She swung her glance away from that bed and walked to look at the *en-suite* bathroom. 'Why should I be disconcerted?' She was striving to sound unconcerned, while inside she was feeling decidedly flurried. Walking into the intimate confines of a double bedroom was the last thing she had expected.

'I don't know; you tell me.' He was teasing her, winding her up and enjoying every moment of it.

She glared at him. 'Maybe it's something to do with your schoolboy sense of humour.'

'*Touché*.' His eyes moved over the slender curves of her body in a thorough appraisal which made her blood race through her veins in confusion.

She turned away from him and looked around the room. 'You certainly like travelling in style.' She made a determined effort to bring things back to a normal level.

'I like anything with style.'

She could feel his eyes still resting on her; it sent a prickly sensation down her spine.

'You've got style, Alexandra,' he said in a low tone.

She turned green eyes back towards him.

'And I'm not referring to the expensive clothes you like to wear, or the education that's been lavished on you. I'm talking about your manner. I like the way you are able to stand up to me, the way you handle yourself. Most women would have acted coy and flirtatious just now, but not you. You are direct, self-assured.'

'That's because I'm not most women; I'm me.' She met his eyes directly.

'You are not what I expected,' he said quietly.

'A spoilt, rich, coy girl?' she asked with a grin.

'Well, there is no doubt that you've been spoilt and that you are not without funds. I suppose that's why I find it so surprising to discover you possess such an independent spirit. As I said before, you're a worthy opponent.'

'You make it sound as if we're going to fight,' she said with a shake of her head.

'Who knows?' For a moment there was silence as they both looked into each other's eyes.

The plane jolted and Alexi put her hand out towards the wall behind her to steady herself. It jolted again and Max reached out to take the champagne glass away from her and place it in the receptacle holders on the table next to him.

She didn't know how it happened, but one moment she was standing next to the bed and the next she was sitting down on it with Max beside her.

'You OK?' he asked softly.

She nodded and watched with a kind of mesmerised interest as his head came closer and his lips tasted hers, gently at first and then with passionate heat. She felt herself leaning back against the softness of the pillows and his hand moving to where the white blouse was tucked into the top of her jeans.

The touch of his hands against the flat planes of her stomach sent a shiver of apprehension and excitement racing in waves through her. She gave herself in to the sheer ecstasy of the moment, curving her fingers up and through his dark hair.

His hands moved up and over her ribcage in a sweeping caress to find the gentle curve of her breast. The sensation made her tingle all over.

He found the front fastener of her bra with unerring, practised ease. It was that and only that which brought her back to her senses.

She forced herself to pull her lips away from the heat of his kiss. 'Max...no.' Her voice was husky and trembling.

He moved back from her immediately. The blue eyes were so intensely blue that they seemed almost electrical.

'I'm sorry.' She pulled her white blouse down with shaking fingers. 'But I can't——'

'It's all right, Alexandra.' He cut across her smoothly and stood up. 'Now is not the right time anyway.' He glanced at his wristwatch and then his eyes moved back over her. 'We'll be landing in San Francisco in about ten minutes. If you want to freshen up in the bathroom, I'll take your drink back to your seat.'

She nodded, grateful for the matter-of-fact tone he was using; it gave her a little time to pull herself together.

She glanced up at him. Beneath that cool, collected tone, she detected an element of fire that told her Max Channing was not as controlled as he would like to be. The notion was vaguely reassuring.

She waited until he turned and left her before she got up from the bed and headed towards the bathroom. She smiled wryly to herself as she studied her reflection in the mirror opposite. One kiss and her cheeks were flushed, her eyes were over-bright, and her legs felt as if they had turned to water. No man had ever had that effect on her before. She had thought a reaction like that was something that only happened to a heroine in a movie.

She splashed her face with cold water and then reapplied her lipstick.

Max Channing was dangerous, she told her reflection sternly. Very dangerous, she thought as she remembered the practised ease with which he had started to unfasten her underwear.

As she turned to leave the bathroom her eyes fell on the two dressing-gowns hung beside the shower. One was undoubtedly Max's, dark blue and monogrammed with his initials. The other was frothy silk, obviously kept for his female guests.

She swallowed hard. She knew Max would probably have no shortage of female company, but somehow knowing that fact and coming face to face with it were two different things. She was mortified to feel a twinge of jealousy for the woman or women who wore that gown. Immediately she dismissed the feeling with an impatient toss of her head. She didn't care how many women were in Max Channing's life; it was nothing to do with her. Her head held high, she returned to her seat.

'Just in time for landing.' Max smiled at her and handed her glass of champagne over. 'To a perfect day out,' he said, raising his glass in a salute.

It was a perfect day in San Francisco. The sun was shining as they strolled together down Fisherman's Wharf.

'I think this is the first time I've been here on such a clear day,' Alexi remarked as she glanced out across the sparkling blue water. 'Usually a thick blanket of mist rolls in and shrouds the bay.'

'Ah, well, I ordered this especially,' Max told her in a droll tone. 'I told the heavens that I was bringing an exceptionally good-looking girl with me to San Francisco and could they please arrange a suitably exceptional day to go with her? And of course when Max Channing puts in an order they wouldn't dare not comply.'

Alexi laughed and shook her head. 'The crazy thing is that I could almost believe that. There's only one problem; if the weather had to be good every time you had a pretty girl on your arm then I'm sure we'd never see a drop of rain.'

'True.' Max grinned and shrugged broad shoulders. 'But you're talking about pretty girls; I'm talking exceptional.' He reached to take hold of her hand. 'And you certainly are that.'

Alexi tried very hard not to be flattered by the compliment. He was a charmer, probably said the same line to half a dozen women a week. The hand that held hers was strong and firm; his thumb caressed the side of her wrist in a gentle movement that sent little flutters of excitement racing through her body, despite the sensible thoughts.

'Come on, let's go and get something to eat.' Max pulled her hand and set off at a brisker pace along the wharf.

Alexi couldn't remember when she had enjoyed a day out or a man's company as much.

The sights and sounds of San Francisco were always a thrill, but today they seemed brighter and fresher. The salt air was heady, the ring of the trolley cars as they moved down the steep streets seemed magical, the sea seemed bluer. And Max...well, Max was exciting. He made her heart beat faster; he made her laugh.

He took her to one of the best seafood restaurants in the area and they dined on lobster thermidor and excellent Californian white wine.

'You like the wine?' Max commented as she remarked for the second time on how good it was. 'It's from a little vineyard in the Napa Valley that I bought last year.'

Alexi stared at him. 'You own a vineyard? I thought that you were more into making films, not wine.'

He shrugged. 'I like to diversify now and then. There's my publishing house in N.Y. and a marina in the South of France and now this little vineyard. I'll take you out there one weekend. I'm sure you would enjoy seeing over the place.' His eyes met hers across the flickering candle-light on the table.

'Sounds interesting,' Alexi replied lightly, while inside a small flurry of tension and excitement burst into life. Max wanted to see her again.

'Perhaps next weekend,' he said smoothly.

'Perhaps,' she murmured cautiously. Tension overtook the thrill of seeing him again as she remembered exactly who she was dealing with. When Maxwell Channing invited a woman away for the weekend there was no doubting that he would expect her to share his bed. She didn't want to be just one more conquest on his list.

Her eyes moved over the broad-shouldered frame, the dark, healthy gleam of his hair, the bright blue of his eyes. This man could really hurt you, Alexi, she told herself sternly. Yet deep in her heart she knew that if he issued the invitation again she would accept.

The knowledge shocked her; she hardly knew the man, for heaven's sake. How on earth could she contemplate having an affair with him?

'Tell me a little about yourself, Max.' She blurted out the question suddenly.

One dark eyebrow lifted and he smiled slightly. 'You know all that's important, surely?'

She smiled at that. 'I know you're single and you like to play the field, but I don't know anything about the real you. For instance, what kind of a childhood did you have? Are your parents alive? That kind of thing.'

For a moment his face clouded over and she didn't think he was going to answer her.

'Let's see, where should I start?' His smile returned, immediately dispelling the thought that she had asked the wrong question. 'My father was American, my mother English; they met when she was over here on holiday and married almost immediately.'

'That's very romantic.' Alexi sipped her coffee and leaned back in her chair.

'They were very much in love. Unfortunately they only had a few years together; she died soon after my seventh birthday.'

Alexi frowned. 'I'm sorry, Max,' she said softly.

He shrugged. 'Anyway, to cut a long story short, my father struggled bringing me up on his own for a while, then a friend of his moved in to help him. She was a woman on her own with a young baby; she had recently left her husband and needed somewhere to stay for a while. There was no romance between them; they were just friends, and it was an arrangement that was mutually beneficial. I had someone to take care of me; she had somewhere to live.'

Alexi nodded. 'And then your father fell in love with her and they married,' she guessed with a smile.

'No, nothing as romantic as that.' He shook his head. 'In fact the story doesn't have a happy ending at all. The woman was only under my father's roof for a mere two months when she had to leave.'

Alexi frowned. 'Why?'

'Her husband decided that she had left him for my father and set out systematically to destroy him.'

'Destroy him?' Alexi stared at him in horror. 'How do you mean?'

'I mean that he financially destroyed him. The man was extremely powerful, had all the right connections. He made sure my father's business folded, then he lost the house...everything that he had worked for.' Max's voice was grim as he told the story; the blue eyes held a glimmer of anger as if he was again reliving what must have been a nightmare.

'That's dreadful, Max.' Alexi shook her head. 'I can't believe someone could be that vindictive.'

For a moment Max was quiet, his eyes moving over the gentle sympathy in her face. 'Can't you...?' He raked a hand through dark hair and then finished his coffee. 'Come on, I'll get the bill and we'll go.'

As soon as they stepped out into the night air the limousine that Max had hired for the day pulled up in front of them and the chauffeur jumped out to open the doors for them.

Max told the chauffeur that they would like to go to the airport as he leaned back in the comfortable seats. Then there was only silence as the powerful car glided through the traffic on the steep roads.

Alexi stole a glance at Max. His strong features were cast into shadow. He looked vulnerable somehow, a word that previously Alexi would never have associated with such a tough man. Her heart went out to him in that instant and impulsively she reached for his hand.

He darted a look of surprise at her. Then his fingers curved around hers and gently he lifted her hand to his lips and kissed it. 'Yes, you are quite a surprise, Alexandra,' he murmured in a husky undertone.

'A good surprise or a bad one?' She grinned up at him, happy now that he was happy again.

'A beautiful one.' His gaze moved over her creamy skin, the vivid green of her eyes, before locking on the generous curve of her lips. 'And I want you very much,' he murmured in an undertone as his lips came down and crushed against hers in a kiss that for a moment was so forceful and so passionate that it left Alexi trembling.

He smiled down at her as he straightened and ran a finger along the contour of her lips.

'I want you to marry me, Alexandra.'

For a moment Alexi thought she had misheard the softly spoken words. She stared up at the dark, handsome features and just couldn't take in what he had said.

He smiled. 'I don't expect an answer right away. Take some time to think it over this week.'

'Max, have you gone crazy?' Her voice was a mere husky whisper.

'Probably,' he said in all seriousness, then grinned.

'But we hardly know each other.' She shook her head, bemused by this sudden development.

'Neither did my parents before they were married, and you seemed to think that story was pretty romantic.'

'But you like to play the field; you told me as much this afternoon. Why on earth——?'

'Alexandra.' He cut across her in a patient tone. 'Believe me, I have given this some thought and I've decided that I want you.'

The car pulled to a smooth halt as it drew up outside the airport, and the chauffeur got out to open the door at Alexi's side.

She made no move. Max was talking as if she were just a new toy he had decided to acquire, like a new car or a new house. He wasn't speaking as if this was a commitment for life, and in Alexi's book that was what marriage was. She stared at him with wide, questioning eyes, feeling too numb to be able to say anything.

'I'm afraid I won't be able to accompany you back. I have some urgent business here in San Francisco tomorrow morning, so I'm going to stay overnight at a hotel.' Max was speaking in a matter-of-fact business tone almost as if the proposal had never occurred. 'But my pilot, Michael, will make sure you get safely home.' He opened his car door and climbed out, leaving Alexi momentarily alone.

'Ah, here is is. Michael, I'll leave Miss Rossini in your capable hands. Make sure you see her safely into the limousine at the other end.'

Hearing Max talking to the other man, Alexi tried to shake off the bemused state she had fallen into, and got out of the car to join them.

Max smiled at her. 'Have a good journey home. I'll speak to you some time next week.' He kissed her cheek briefly. She could smell the warm, tangy scent of his cologne as he bent near, and for one instant she wanted to slide her arms up and around his neck; she wanted him to hold her. He turned and got back into the limousine.

Alexi watched it pull out into the main flow of traffic. She didn't understand Max Channing at all. Why on earth had he proposed to her? He wasn't in love with her; how could he be? He hardly knew her. He was a loner, a man who liked to change his women almost as often as his cars. Why would he want to give up that lifestyle for her?

'If you are ready, Ms Rossini?'

The young pilot's voice coming from her elbow made her realise that she had been staring towards the limo long after it had disappeared.

She turned with a start. 'Yes, I am.'

As they walked into the airport terminal the man made polite conversation about the weather, about San Francisco. Alexandra was hardly listening. All she could think about was Max. Why had he proposed? There had to be an ulterior motive somewhere.

CHAPTER FIVE

'HAVE you seen today's society column?' Miles enquired in a dry tone as he sauntered into Alexi's office early Friday morning.

'Yes, I've seen it.' Alexi strove to sound uninterested as she flicked through the files in front of her.

'And?'

'And what?' Alexi looked up at him, a deliberately blank look on her face.

'And you must have some opinion on the write-up,' Miles went on, totally disregarding the fact that his colleague obviously didn't want to discuss the matter. 'After all, it was about your father's live-in girlfriend having a wonderful time out on the town with Max Channing. Two people you have a special interest in.'

'I wouldn't say I had a special interest in either of them,' Alexi muttered, bending her head back to her work. 'Monica is simply my father's girlfriend and Max is just a friend.'

'Just a friend who took you out last weekend to San Francisco,' Miles remarked with a shrug of his shoulders. 'We'll forget the fact that all you talked about on Monday was Max Channing. We had, ''What do you think of him, Miles? Do you think he plans to stay in this country? Do you know why he's over here?'' It was practically your sole source of conversation,' he said in a sardonic tone.

'Don't exaggerate, Miles,' she said crossly. 'We had a pleasant day out, end of story. As for the article in today's newspaper, I've learned from experience never to believe all I read. It was only last week that Georgia Gold was implying that there was something going on between Monica and Robert.'

'So you're not upset?'

'Of course I'm not upset. Stop fretting, Miles.'

'OK.' He smiled good-naturedly. 'So you do intend to follow up that business call that Channing made on Wednesday asking for someone to call out to the house with a view of refurbishing?'

'Yes, of course,' she answered crisply. 'Now, do you think we could turn our thoughts to something a little more important, like our accounts?' She leafed through the files in front of her, searching in a businesslike way for the relevant information. She didn't want to discuss Max Channing. 'I notice that three of our major accounts from last month haven't paid us yet.'

Miles nodded his head gravely. 'Reminder notices have been sent out, but there is still no sign of them paying up. That's part of the reason I'm so keen for you to chase up the Channing account; we need all the fresh work we can get.'

'All right, Miles, point taken. Please don't harp on about Max Channing.' She glanced up at him, an unconsciously pleading light in her green eyes.

He shrugged. 'All right, Alexi, but don't forget that our contractors are waiting to be paid, and they're hefty bills this month. Mrs Thomas had all her settees recovered in Chinese silk, and Ted Major had mosaic flooring put in, to name just a few little items. Not to mention the fact that our dreaded lease is up for renewal.'

'Don't panic, we'll probably get paid today and new work is always flooding in. As for the lease, I'm sure it won't go up that much, and if it does I'll find the money,' she said with determination.

'You may find the money, but I won't,' Miles muttered gloomily.

'Don't be silly; as long as we have the money it doesn't matter who gets it. Don't be so negative.'

'Oh, no, Alexi, I'm not playing at that. Either I come up with my share or I'm afraid I'll have to opt out of the business.' Miles sounded really depressed now.

Alexi glanced up at her friend. There was a proud, stubborn look on his face that told her it was no use arguing the point. She could hardly blame him for wanting to be completely independent; after all, she was the same. Many a time her father had offered to put money into the business, and she had always refused.

She found it hard to settle to her work after that depressing conversation. Contrary to what she had said to cheer Miles up, she was worried about the late payments from several of their clients; it was a tremendous strain on their resources. She was also more than a little annoyed with Maxwell Channing.

What kind of a man proposed to a woman and then didn't bother to ring her for a week? What kind of a man proposed and then dated another woman in the same week? The questions ran around and around in her brain with tormenting frequency.

The fact that he had rung the office on business and hadn't even asked to speak to her angered her even more. What kind of a game was the man playing?

Now there was this article in the paper about him and Monica Houston. Obviously she was the reason he hadn't been in contact, and it made Alexi blazing mad. Not because she was jealous, she told herself heatedly now, but because Monica was supposed to be in love with her father, and what would Henri Rossini say? Would he be hurt? She had the feeling that he would, and she couldn't stand that.

Alex glared at the work in front of her. Just who did Max Channing think he was? she wondered furiously. She had a good mind to go out there and tell him exactly what she thought about his womanising ways. She glanced at her watch and then on impulse got to her feet. That was exactly what she would do, go out there and give him a piece of her mind.

It wasn't until she had driven up in front of his house that common sense returned. How could she in all honesty lecture a prospective client about his moral behaviour? Firstly, it was none of her business whom he dated. It wasn't as if she was engaged to him; he might have proposed, but she hadn't accepted. And secondly, they needed his business.

Her lips curved in the first real smile of the day at such a mercenary thought. Times must be bad, she thought sarcastically, if she was prepared to swallow her principles and deal with the man in a courteous manner, because she had just decided that he was a total rat.

She stepped out of the Lamborghini and walked up the steps to his front door. The air was warm with the tang of salt carried on a small breeze over the ocean. The only sound was the cackling cry of a seagull from the roof of the house. He sounds as if he's laughing at me, Alexi thought idly as she waited for the doorbell to be answered. He sounds as if he knows something I don't, as if he's saying, You fool, keep away from that door. She shook off the fanciful thought as the door swung open and Rosie, the housekeeper, welcomed her with a smile.

'Good morning, Miss Rossini. Mr Channing has been expecting you. Please come in.'

'Thank you.' She followed the woman into the house. Had Max really been expecting her? she wondered. Even though he hadn't spoken a word to her all week? Maybe he thought she was the type of woman to seize the excuse of coming to discuss work just to see him again. If that was the case he was even more conceited than she had thought.

'Mr Channing is in his study. If you'd like to wait here a moment I'll just go through and ask if it's convenient for you to go in.' She left Alexi standing in the wide hallway, and then came back out a moment later.

'Please go in,' she said holding the door open.

Alexi stepped past her with a feeling of trepidation, though why she should feel nervous about seeing Max again she had no idea.

The room that she entered was very masculine in its design, the carpets dark beige, the walls lined completely with books. Max sat behind a huge desk, his dark head resting back against the cream leather of his chair.

'Ah, Alexandra, it's good to see you.' His eyes moved over her slender body in the businesslike suit in a way that made her blood-pressure increase dramatically.

'Good morning, Max.' Her voice was cool.

'Please take a seat.' He waved her towards the chair opposite and then as she sat down got up to walk towards the table behind him. 'Coffee?' He held up the coffee-pot questioningly and then as she nodded poured two cups and brought them back.

He was dressed in a dark grey suit that fitted the broad-shouldered frame perfectly. He looked too handsome for Alexi's peace of mind.

She picked up the delicate china cup and sipped the coffee. It was exactly as she liked it. Max was the kind of person who paid attention to detail; he remembered how she liked her coffee, and she had the distinct feeling that he noticed all the tell-tale signs and knew exactly how nervous she was feeling right at this moment.

'So...' He lingered over the word thoughtfully as his eyes moved over the pale features, the dark gloss of her hair. 'Is this a personal visit or a business one?'

The direct question startled her. She had expected him to presume instantly that she come to see him on a distinctly personal basis.

'I believe you would like your house redesigning?' she asked crisply.

He smiled and leaned back lazily against his chair. 'That's correct. I spoke to Thornton about it on Wednesday.'

She nodded. 'Miles would have come out to look the place over himself, but he's tied up until next week.' She tried very hard to make it clear that she hadn't come by choice.

'Well, I'm very glad that he is tied up,' Max drawled, a gleam of amusement lurking for a moment in his blue eyes. 'Because it was your expertise and taste that I was hoping for.'

There was an awkward silence for just a moment as Alexi strove to find a suitable reply to that. 'So what exactly have you got in mind?' She decided to ignore the comment entirely and cut directly to the work involved.

He shrugged. 'That's entirely up to you. I'll give you a free hand to do exactly what you would like to the place. When you've finished your coffee I'll give you a tour over everything.'

Alexi nodded and picked up the china cup again. She wished she hadn't said she would have a coffee. She just wanted to get this ordeal over.

'Perhaps you would like to stay and have some lunch with me afterwards?' The invitation was spoken in a casual tone, but it instantly made Alexi stiffen.

'No, thank you. I have another appointment.' Her voice was remarkably cool, considering the turmoil inside her. She had no appointment, but if he thought that he could pick her up and then drop her as the whim took him he could think again. The man had a nerve, an unmitigated nerve. How could he sit there so cool, as if he had never even taken her out, let alone proposed to her?

'In that case we had better get started,' he said smoothly. There was no hint of any kind of emotion in his voice. There was no way she could tell what might be going through his mind. He certainly didn't seem bothered by her refusal, but then again he was a businessman, and to Max Channing it would probably be the norm to put business before pleasure.

He got to his feet and she hastily put her cup down and joined him. 'As I said, you can have a free hand with the house, but there is one exception and that is this room,' Max told her crisply. 'This is my domain; I do a lot of work in here and don't want the upheaval and inconvenience of having decorators around me.'

'That's fine,' Alexi murmured, and opened her handbag to take out her notebook and pen.

'Everything else is up to you.' Max opened the door and strode down the corridor. The doors that he opened along the way all led into the most luxurious bedrooms with bathrooms *en suite*. The place looked as if it had been decorated quite recently, and very tastefully decorated at that.

'This is my bedroom.' Max opened the last door at the end of the corridor.

Alexi would have known it was his bedroom immediately. It was totally masculine, almost to the point of being severe, yet the underlying feel to the décor was overtly sexual. A huge water-bed dominated the centre of the room, black and white satin-silk covers adorning it. Heavy black furniture that was exquisitely hand-carved broke the starkness of white walls and white carpet.

'I think a few feminine touches are called for in here.' Max turned to her, a grin lighting up the contours of his face. 'How do you feel about water-beds?'

Alexi tried very hard not to look as disconcerted as she felt. 'Personally I don't care for them.'

'So you have slept on one before?' Max continued, a teasing gleam in the bright blue of his eyes.

Alexi frowned. She had actually never slept on one, but she didn't think that was any of his business. 'I think that your question is completely inappropriate,' she answered him crisply. 'I'm here to see to the business of redesigning your décor, not to give you my personal observations.'

'No?' One eyebrow lifted sardonically. 'I thought that your personal observations were exactly what I was paying for.'

She could feel herself flushing now. Damn the man, he was able to throw her off balance too easily. 'Yes...but this is your room, your house. I want to do it to your taste, not mine.' She bent her head towards her notebook as she spoke, pretending to be busy jotting down information.

'Am I to take it from that statement that you are not considering the prospect of coming to live here?'

The quietly asked question made her head jerk up in surprise. Their eyes met and held for an instant before Alexi lowered hers again in complete consternation. 'To be honest with you, Max, I never gave the idea a moment's thought.' Liar, a little voice whispered inside her; she had done nothing but think about it. 'I had the impression that your proposal was some kind of a whim, or that you were joking or something.' She wished her voice didn't sound so breathless.

'Well, then you must think I have a very strange sense of humour,' he retorted drily.

She looked up from her notepad and their eyes met again. The look in that intense blue gaze sent a tremor racing through her. 'I don't know what to think,' she answered softly. That at least was the truth. She had never been so completely at a loss. 'When you didn't ring me this week, I could only presume that you weren't serious. Then there was that article about you and Monica.' Why on earth had she mentioned that? she wondered frantically. Now he was going to think that she was jealous.

The firm mouth slanted in a half-smile. 'Is that why you're annoyed with me?'

'I am not annoyed with you,' she denied heatedly.

'No?' One eyebrow lifted mockingly. 'You're certainly acting as if you're annoyed with me. Very cool, very businesslike.'

'That's because I'm here on business,' she snapped.

'Nothing to do with the fact that you're jealous?' he asked drolly.

'Of course not!' Despite all her efforts to the contrary, her cheeks flooded a bright crimson red. 'I have absolutely no reason to be jealous.'

'Now that is true.' He smiled and stepped forwards, and then much to Alexandra's consternation he reached out a hand and tipped her chin up. 'You have absolutely no reason to be jealous of Monica Houston because there is nothing going on between us.' His thumb gently caressed the soft skin at her jawline as he spoke, sending a shiver racing through her. 'She happened to be seated next to me at a dinner party and later she was asking me about the British film industry. I think she's interested in a new film we're just starting to cast for.'

'I don't care what you were talking about, or what happened; it's none of my business.' She swung her head away from him, her heart pounding.

'And the reason I didn't speak to you when I rang your office,' he continued on as if she had never spoken, 'was that I didn't want you to think the work I want doing was connected to your accepting my proposal. I don't want to pressurise you in any way, Alexandra,' he added gently. 'But I do want you to say yes.'

She looked up into blue eyes. He was serious; she hadn't let herself believe it until now. The realisation sent shivers racing through her. Shivers of excitement, shivers of apprehension.

'How about having dinner with me tonight?' he invited softly. 'We can talk some more and——'

There was a tap on the open door behind them. 'Sorry to disturb you, Mr Channing, but there is a Ms Houston here to see you.' Rosie's voice interrupted the intimate murmur of his voice.

'All right, Rosie, I'll be through in a moment,' Max said smoothly. 'So how about it, Alexandra—dinner tonight?' he asked as if there had been no interruption.

Alexi couldn't think straight. She wanted to have dinner with him, but she had the distinct feeling that she was getting out of her depth with Max Channing. And why was Monica waiting to see him?

Aware that he was waiting for an answer and that the silence was stretching, she shook her head. 'I can't tonight, Max. I shall be working late at the office. Maybe another evening.'

He nodded. 'All right, another evening,' he agreed smoothly, then glanced at his watch. 'I suppose we should go and see Monica.'

Monica was in the front lounge, standing at the windows, looking out over the blue of the ocean. Her figure was a perfect silhouette against the background of sea and sky, curvaceous, yet petite, in riding breeches and a white lace-up top. Her blonde hair was loose and flowing around the delicate oval face.

'Max, darling.' She turned fully as she heard them come in. Then her eyes narrowed slightly as they took in Alexi. 'Alexi, this is a surprise! Are you not working today?'

'Alexandra has come out to cast her professional eye over this place, Monica. I'm hoping she's going to transform it for me,' Max explained smoothly.

Monica smiled, once more perfectly relaxed. 'Oh, I'm sure she will, darling; she's marvellous. And if you need a second opinion on anything at any time you only need to ask me.'

'Well, that's very kind of you.' Max smiled and turned to the drinks cabinet beside him. 'Can I offer you some refreshment? Iced tea . . . or maybe something stronger?'

'Iced tea would be lovely.' Monica crossed and sat down in the centre of the large settee. 'I really called to see if you would like to accompany me on a ride this afternoon, Max. I remembered you telling me how much you like riding back in England, and I thought as it's such a wonderful day . . .' Monica let her voice trail invitingly.

'Sounds great.' Max came around and handed her the drink. 'But unfortunately I do have some business to attend to this afternoon.'

'Oh, what a shame!' She gave him a provocative look up through long dark lashes. 'It would have been such fun.'

Alexi cringed at the blatantly flirtatious manner.

'How about dinner this evening, then, Max? I would very much like to carry on our discussion from the other evening,' the woman continued confidently.

'How about staying for lunch instead?' Max invited with a smile.

Monica cast an uncertain glance at Alexi; obviously she was wondering whether lunch was going to be a threesome.

'I have to get back to the office, Monica,' Alexi told her in a dry tone.

'That is a pity.' The tone of regret was completely insincere. Monica was obviously delighted that it would

just be her and Max. She leaned back against the soft
cushions, and scarlet lips curved in a bright smile. 'In
that case I should love to stay and keep you company,
darling.' There was a light in the blue eyes that said she
would keep him company all afternoon and well into the
night given half a chance.

'Alexandra, would you like some iced tea?' Max
turned towards her, catching the brief look of disdain
on her face.

'No, thank you, I have to be going,' she answered him
stiffly. 'So if you'll excuse me...' As she spoke she made
her way towards the door.

'I'll see you out.' Max moved with her across the room.

When he opened the door she said goodbye to him in
a brief, clipped tone. He made no reply; instead he
walked outside with her. When she slanted a surprised
look up at him he smiled. 'I'll walk you to your car.'

'There's no need, thank you.'

'Do lighten up, Alexandra,' he said with a shake of
his head.

Long dark hair swung back as she glared up at him.
'What is that supposed to mean?'

'It means you're acting like a jealous woman, and I've
told you there is no romance brewing between me and
Monica. So you can stop giving me those frosty, disapproving looks.'

'If you think I am in any way bothered about you and
Monica then you are sadly mistaken,' she bit back
sharply. 'I hope you enjoy your lunch with her,' she
added in a softer tone. It irritated her beyond words that
he should think she cared enough to be jealous.

'Thank you.' He sounded highly amused now, and
that irritated her even further.

They stopped next to the sleek lines of the
Lamborghini. His eyes moved over her slender figure as
she leaned slightly back against its door and looked up

at him. 'When would you like us to get started on the work to your house?' she asked, deciding to bring the conversation swiftly back to business. It seemed the safest course of action.

'As soon as you can,' he replied easily.

'We didn't discuss money,' she remembered now with a frown. 'What kind of a budget do you want us to work to?'

'Alexandra, honey...' he drawled with a half-smile. 'I really don't give a damn how much it costs, just as long as you do a good job.'

'I see.' Alexi turned and opened the car door. 'We always do a good job, Max,' she told him over her shoulder.

'Glad to hear it.' He watched her climb in behind the driving-wheel, his eyes momentarily lingering on the slender length of her legs before she pushed her skirt down a little with hands that weren't entirely steady. She wished he wouldn't look at her like that; it totally unnerved her.

'So when will you come back to me?' he asked softly.

'Sorry?' She looked up at him with puzzled green eyes. Was he talking about business or was there a personal note to that question?

'When will you get back to me with your ideas?' he asked with a grin.

'As soon as I can.' She flared the engine into life, eager to be away. She couldn't even manage to have an ordinary conversation with this man without feeling there were sexual undertones lurking to confuse and trap her.

'Good, because I hate waiting for something once I've made up my mind that I want it. I tend to grow impatient.' He shook his head and there was a gleam in his eyes that made a shiver run through her. 'And when I get impatient there is no telling what I will do.'

Her hands tightened on the steering-wheel. He was teasing her, winding her up, she decided. Although he was looking at her quite seriously now, a strangely watchful expression on his handsome features. 'I'll get straight on to it, Max,' she told him and then with a nod she put her foot down and accelerated down and out of his drive.

She felt strangely breathless as she drove back along the coast. The beauty of the sea and the scenery around her were lost on her. She was plagued with snatches of that conversation playing through her mind. Max telling her that he was serious about wanting to marry her, Max telling her that he didn't like waiting for something once he had made up his mind that he wanted it.

Why had he asked her to marry him? She asked herself the question over and over again. He hadn't said he loved her... He did desire her, though. She remembered the look in his eyes as he had run them over her body; the memory made her temperature increase dramatically.

She slowed the car and pulled it in at the next lay-by. She was breathing fast and her heart was racing. It was totally ridiculous that the man could affect her like this.

At this moment now he would be sitting across the table from Monica, no doubt making her blood race like molten lava every time he smiled. Would he be flirting with her? Would he be asking her to join him this evening for dinner? The idea made her boiling mad, and it was nothing to do with the fact that Monica was her father's girlfriend. She was jealous; the realisation struck her suddenly. She didn't want to think of Max flirting with another woman, and the idea that he might kiss her later made her stomach muscles clench as if someone had just punched her.

She leaned her head back against the seat and closed her eyes, willing herself to get things back into perspective. She couldn't be in love with Max... She hardly knew him, yet she had never felt such an overwhelming attraction for any man. She wished now that she hadn't turned down his invitation for dinner tonight. She wanted to see him; she couldn't understand the conflicting emotions tearing her apart inside. She wanted so much to see him, yet she was so afraid of seeing him.

She opened her eyes and looked out over the ocean. Just what was it she was afraid of? She tried to face her fears rationally. Was it that she might be hurt? She did tend to be naturally wary where men were concerned. There had been so many of her boyfriends who hadn't really been interested in her as a person, but in who she was. Martin, for instance; he had been more interested in the fact that she was Henri Rossini's daughter than he had been in her, and he had successfully managed to get a much prized part in one of Henri's films as a result.

But Max was different; he was a very wealthy powerful man in his own right. When he had said that he wanted her, he must have been sincere—there could be no ulterior motives. He would hardly be interested in her father's money or gaining a part in her father's films. He wanted her, nothing more than that. The thought created a warm feeling inside her. There had never been a time when she was sure that someone was just attracted to her and not who she was. Feeling happier than she had in a long time, she started the car engine and headed back for the office.

It was the following week before she heard anything from Max again. She walked into her office early Monday morning to find it filled with flowers. The heavy scent of blood-red roses combined with white orchids enveloped the small room, taking her breath away.

'Beautiful, aren't they?' Her secretary came in behind her with a smile. 'I put the card and the package that accompanied them on your desk.'

'Thank you, Jenny.' Alexi moved to take her seat behind the desk. Her eyes moved over the small package beautifully wrapped in silver paper and tied with a red ribbon. A silver envelope sat on top of it, her name written across it in a flowing hand. Taking the paper-knife from the drawer beside her, she slit it open.

The silver card inside read: 'Dinner tonight? Max.'

Alexi smiled; the man certainly didn't waste words. Then she opened the package sitting next to her.

Silver paper revealed a box with the Cartier name inscribed across it. Inside was a ruby and diamond pendant on a thick gold rope. Alexi stared at it in surprise; it was exquisite and must have cost a fortune. She took it from the box and it caught the light from the window, flashing a fiery red more brilliant than the roses around her.

'Wow!' Miles walked into her office and stopped dead. 'Some guy is obviously out to impress. Nancy is lucky if she gets a box of candy from me.' He walked towards her and leaned against her desk with a grin. 'Let me guess . . . Max Channing?'

She nodded and put the necklace back in the box.

'He must be serious.'

'I don't know.' Alexi shrugged and slipped the box away into the top drawer of her desk. 'He's asked me to marry him.' She hadn't intended to say anything about that, but somehow it just slipped out. She needed to talk to someone about it. She slanted a look up at her friend and smiled as she saw the thunderstruck expression on his face.

'No wonder you weren't worried about those silly articles in the gossip column.' He shook his head and regained his composure. 'It's wonderful, Alexi!' The handsome face split into a wide grin. 'I'm so pleased for you.'

She held up a hand. 'Not so fast, Miles; I haven't said yes.'

He frowned. 'Why not?'

'Miles, I hardly know the guy.'

He smiled. 'I hardly knew Nancy when I proposed to her. But I knew the moment I saw her that she was the girl for me.'

'I don't know, Miles.' She pushed a trembling hand through long dark hair. 'I'm very attracted to him...but I just don't know.'

He reached out and tipped her chin upwards. 'You are more than just attracted to the guy, Alexi...you're crazy about him. I can see it in your eyes... You light up every time his name is mentioned.'

She looked away from him, feeling a little embarrassed. 'But I'm not sure about him, Miles...about how he feels.'

'I'd say it's pretty damn obvious how he feels,' Miles said drily, glancing around at the room full of flowers. 'Listen, Alexi, Max Channing is probably the hottest catch in town. A million women would die to be in the position you're in, but he's chosen you. I'd say that means he's fallen for you...and fallen hard. Don't throw away the opportunity for happiness just because you're frightened to take a chance.'

Those words kept playing through Alexi's mind all morning. She was frightened, she freely admitted that, but wasn't it better to be cautious about such a big commitment?

Then just before lunch Max walked into her office and all caution just seemed to fly away. He looked so handsome, the firm lips twisted in a half-smile as his gaze travelled slowly over her pale skin, the delicate beauty of the blooms surrounding her. 'I see you received my gift.'

She nodded. 'Thank you.' For a moment there was silence. She felt self-conscious for some reason. It was strange how Max had that effect on her; he made her feel like an awkward teenager aware of her body and her looks for the first time. 'I was going to ring you at lunchtime and thank you,' she added lamely.

'And accept my invitation to dinner, I hope?' he added. There was supreme confidence in his tone.

She hesitated for a second. 'Has any woman ever dared to refuse you anything?' She lifted her chin a little higher and met his eyes.

There was a gleam of humour in the blue depths at the note of challenge. He pursed his lips and seemed to consider the question for a moment. 'No... I don't believe they have.' He grinned. 'Certainly no one has given me so much of a run-around as you have these last few days.'

Alexi could believe it. In all probability women usually melted into his arms. He would never have had to ask twice for a date.

He crossed the floor towards her. 'The strange thing is, the more you turn me down... the more I'm determined to have you.'

Alexi fidgeted uneasily with her pen as he came closer around her desk. 'Maybe I should turn your invitation down, then?' She slanted a look up at him that was unconsciously provocative.

'I don't think so, Alexandra. You've played all the games I'm going to allow.' He reached out a hand and took the pen from her hand, then slowly he pulled her to her feet.

'Did you like the little trinket I sent with the flowers?' he asked smoothly.

She smiled; the little trinket had probably cost a small fortune. 'Oh, you mean the fake diamonds and the paste red stone?' she enquired with a teasing light in her green eyes.

'That's the one.' He went along with her in an indulgent tone. 'Were the fake diamonds not big enough?'

'Not nearly.' She smiled up at him, her eyes telling him a completely different story.

He traced a light finger down the side of her cheek, his eyes taking in every detail of her appearance. 'Well, I'm sorry about that, Alexandra,' he said in a low tone. 'Because I do believe that only the best is good enough for you.' He put his hand down and reached into the inside pocket of his lightweight jacket. 'How about this, then . . . ?' He brought out a small ring box and held it out towards her.

She hesitated for a moment before taking it. Her heart was beating double time and her hands weren't entirely steady as she opened it. Inside was the most beautiful ring she had ever seen—a large solitaire diamond set in a twist of gold.

'The jeweller assured me that it's flawless,' Max told her as she made no attempt to take it out of the box. 'A flawless ring for my flawless beauty…hmm?' He took the box from her nerveless fingers and picked the ring out. He held it up to the light so that its brilliant sparkle flared to life. Then he looked at her, one dark eyebrow lifted in question. 'What do you say, Alexandra?'

Alexi didn't know what to say. She wanted very much to ask him if he loved her. But she didn't dare risk such a question.

He lifted her left hand and placed the ring on her finger with a gentle yet positive movement. It fitted perfectly. 'Meant for you.' He smiled into the deep green of her eyes. 'Say you'll be my wife, Alexandra.' The husky deep voice made the request sound like a command.

She stared into the vivid blue of his gaze. His eyes were the blue of the sea on a tranquil summer day. Lazily inviting, they stared back at her. A girl could drown in those eyes, she thought hazily.

'Alexandra?' he prompted her, the deep voice velvet-smooth.

What would happen if she said no? she wondered for a second. Would he go away back to England and never see her again? The thought was surprisingly painful; she couldn't stand never to see him again. She was in love with him.

She shook her head wonderingly as the realisation hit her. She didn't know when it had happened, but she was in love with this man.

For a second the handsome features clouded over. 'Is that a definite no, Alexandra?' he asked, and there was a bleak note to his voice that made her heart sing. He did love her...he cared very much about her answer.

She smiled up at him. 'It's a definite yes, Max,' she told him softly. 'Yes, I will marry you.'

The firm lips curved in a smile and there was a light in those eyes that was almost triumphant. He lifted her hand and touched it gently to his lips, but there was no passionate kiss. 'Next week,' he told her in a husky tone.

'Sorry?' She frowned, not understanding him.

'Next week we'll be married.' He released her hand and smiled down at her.

'Next week?' She laughed in startled amusement. 'Surely you're joking?'

'I've never been more serious. Next week we'll have a quiet little service at a chapel in L.A., and you will become Mrs Max Channing.'

She frowned. 'I don't understand the rush, Max. I need more time to get things——'

'You don't need more time, Alexandra. I don't want you changing your mind,' he told her firmly.

She smiled at that. 'I won't change my mind, Max.'

'No?' One dark eyebrow lifted and he smiled. 'I'm glad to hear it... Even so, I think we should be married as soon as possible. The longer we leave it the more people will find out about it, and instead of a quiet service we'll be mobbed by the media. They always turn things like this into a three-ring circus event.'

'Maybe.' She shook her head thoughtfully. 'I agree I'd like a quiet service. But I'll have to wait until my father comes home; he'll want——'

'No, Alexandra. It will be you and me and a couple of witnesses,' he interrupted her with decision. Then he kissed her lips. It was a kiss of determination, strong, passionate; it completely took her breath away. 'Next week,' he told her as he lifted his head.

'Next week,' she repeated, her mind whirling in a crazy haze of intense longing.

CHAPTER SIX

'ALEXI, are you ready? It's nearly...' Nancy broke off as she entered Alexi's bedroom and saw her standing in front of the mirror. 'You look gorgeous,' she breathed in genuine admiration.

'Do you think so?' Alexi turned apprehensively to face Miles's wife.

The other woman smiled as her eyes moved over her friend's appearance. The champagne silk dress fitted perfectly to the curves of Alexi's lovely figure and finished above the knee, showing the shapely long legs to their best advantage. Her dark hair was caught back from the delicate oval face and cascaded over her shoulders in glossy curls.

'I don't think so...I know so. Max is going to be completely bowled over when he sees you at that church.' She glanced at her watch. 'Which will be in about twenty minutes' time. So we had better get a move on.'

Panic stirred inside Alexi at those words. Twenty minutes' time and she would be Mrs Maxwell Channing. Was she doing the right thing? The niggling doubts returned to plague her. She hardly knew Maxwell Channing.

It was just over a week now since he had proposed to her, and although she had dined with him either at lunch or dinner every day she still felt no nearer to really knowing him.

'You all right, Alexi?' Nancy asked as she caught the tense expression on her friend's face.

Alexi nodded. 'A little apprehensive,' she admitted in a husky tone. 'It's all happened so fast and I was just thinking that Max is really still a stranger to me. I'm not a hundred per cent sure about him.'

Nancy laughed. 'I remember thinking the same thing when I married Miles, and I had been seeing him for nearly a year before. There is always that element of doubt, Alexi. I don't think you ever really know someone until you've lived with them.'

'I suppose you're right,' Alexi conceded. 'At least I know that Max is marrying me because he wants *me*, not because I'm Henri Rossini's daughter. That's all a lot of men are interested in.'

Nancy shot a look of disbelief at her friend. 'I'm sure that's not the only thing your boyfriends have been interested in. You are a very beautiful girl, Alexi.'

Alexi shrugged. 'Believe me, Nancy, a lot of men just have an eye for the main chance, whether it be money or a break for their acting career.'

For a moment Nancy's dark eyes clouded with worry. 'You don't still have a thing about Martin, do you?'

'Martin?' For a moment the question startled Alexi. She hardly ever thought about her ex-boyfriend. Martin Steel had been just a friend; she had never been serious about him. 'Certainly not,' she said with the utmost assurance.

'That's all right, then.' Her friend's pretty features relaxed into a smile. 'It was just when you mentioned a break in an acting career it made me think of him——'

'And you thought I was still smarting about the way I was used and that maybe I was marrying on the rebound?' Alexi finished for her with a rueful grin. Then more seriously she added, 'No, Nancy, I never felt about Martin the way I feel about Max. If I thought Max had an underhand ulterior motive for marrying me I wouldn't just be a little upset—I'd be devastated.'

The two girls headed out of the door and downstairs as they spoke.

'Well, I wouldn't worry, Alexi,' Nancy said with a smile. 'Maxwell Channing is a very wealthy, very powerful man. He certainly doesn't need to marry for any other reason than love.'

Did Max love her? The silent question raced around and around inside her with painful intensity. He had never said that he loved her.

She picked up her bouquet from the hall table. White carnations surrounded by frothy white baby's breath. She tilted her head down towards its sweet fragrance and for just a moment she was torn with deep anguish. Everything would have been all right if only Max had told her he loved her. There would be no doubt in her mind about marrying him, because she knew that she loved him, she knew it with every fibre of her body.

She glanced up and her eyes met Nancy's. 'I wish my father was here,' she said softly.

Nancy nodded in understanding. 'Did you try to contact him?'

Alexi nodded. 'I phoned three times and left messages for him, but he hasn't returned my calls.'

Nancy linked her arm through her friend's. 'He probably hasn't even received your messages. You know what he's like when he's working. You didn't hear anything from him for nearly ten months when he was filming in the Caribbean.'

'Yes, I know what he's like,' Alexi said softly as they went out of the door.

Max was waiting outside the church with Miles when they arrived. Both men looked extremely attractive in grey morning suits and blue silk cravats. But it was Max who held Alexi's full attention. He looked so dynamic, his raven-black hair neatly styled, the vivid flame-blue eyes trained solely on her as she stepped out of the car.

'You look fabulous,' Miles told her with a smile.

She pulled her gaze away from Max for a moment to smile back at her friend. Then she looked back at Max, an unconsciously vulnerable expression on her young face as she waited for him to say something.

He smiled. 'I'm a very lucky man,' he said with a husky drawl that caught her heart-strings and made the blood thunder through her veins in a molten hot wave of emotion. Then he reached out and caught her small hand in his large one to squeeze it gently. 'Let's make this legal, shall we?'

The service was over almost before it had begun. They exchanged vows in the small church, their only witnesses Miles and Nancy. Then Max slipped the gold band on to her finger and she was Mrs Maxwell Channing.

It was almost like a dream. He kissed her gently then they walked back out into the bright glare of the summer sun and Nancy was showering them with confetti.

Max's limousine was waiting for them and all four were taken back to one of L.A.'s most prestigious restaurants for a wedding breakfast.

Alexi came to an abrupt halt as they walked into the restaurant and discovered that it was empty. Usually the place was heaving with people, especially at this time of day. She turned questioning eyes up to her husband.

'I decided it was a good idea just to book the whole restaurant,' he told her with a grin. 'I think we deserve a bit of privacy on such a momentous occasion.'

Nancy's eyes widened at such an extravagant gesture, but before anyone could say anything the head waiter came across to greet them.

They were shown towards one of the alcoves where a table had been laid in preparation, two ice buckets cooling Alexi's favourite Dom Pérignon.

'You think of everything,' Alexi said as he popped the corks and filled four flute glasses with the sparkling liquid.

'I hope so.' Max lifted his glass in salute. 'To my beautiful bride.'

'To the beautiful bride.' Both Miles and Nancy lifted their glasses to the toast.

'And to the two wonderful witnesses,' Alexi said with a grin, taking a sip of her champagne.

'It was our pleasure,' Miles said smoothly. 'I hope that you'll both be very happy.'

'Thanks, Miles.' She smiled at her friend with genuine gratitude.

'So where are you off to for your honeymoon? Or is it a secret?' Miles enquired, taking another sip of his drink and relaxing back in his chair.

'No secret,' Max answered directly. 'I'm taking Alexandra to stay at my vineyard in the Napa Valley for a couple of days.'

'Only a couple of days?' Miles glanced towards Alexi with a frown. 'I thought that you were away for at least a week.'

'So did I.' Alexi looked questioningly at Max and he shrugged.

'Sorry, honey. I just heard this morning that I need to be in New York next week on a matter of urgent business. So we'll have to cut the honeymoon short. I hope you don't mind.'

Alexi did mind. It was the kind of thing that her father would have done; he also always put business first. 'Couldn't your business have waited until after our honeymoon?' she asked crisply.

He shook his head. 'Afraid not.'

The waiter arrived to take their order and the subject was dropped. But inside Alexi was hurt that Max could inform her that their honeymoon was to be cut short in such a casual manner.

'Where are you and Alexi going to live when you get back from the honeymoon?' Nancy asked a little later as they ate dinner.

'My house at Malibu beach,' Max said easily. 'I was going to ask you, Miles, if you would get in contact with that real estate agency who wanted to buy Alexandra's house. Tell them that the owner has changed her mind about selling and will be in contact on her return——'

'Hold on a moment, Max,' Alexi cut across him abruptly. 'I don't remember saying that I was going to sell my house.'

Max frowned. 'We discussed this the other night, Alexandra, and I remember distinctly that you agreed that we should live at the beach house.'

'Well…yes,' Alexi agreed hesitantly. They had talked briefly about where they should live. She had mainly wanted to know if Max wanted to go back to England and had been relieved to find he had no immediate plans to return. 'But I didn't say I was going to sell my house.'

One dark eyebrow lifted and there was a clear expression of displeasure on Max's face for just a moment. 'It's just not practical to keep that house, Alexandra; we don't need it. I have a house here, a house in London, an apartment in New York, not to mention the vineyard. What on earth do we want that large house of yours for?'

There was an awkward silence for just a moment. Alexi knew he was right—it probably wasn't practical to keep the house—yet she was loath to sell it for some reason.

Then she shrugged. 'I suppose you have a point, Max. All right, Miles, if you wouldn't mind ringing the agency, and I'll deal with it when we get back.'

The rest of the meal passed with just light-hearted conversation. Sometimes Max could be utterly charming,

Alexi thought as she listened to him talking to Nancy. Her friend obviously thought he was wonderful; she was hanging on his every word and throwing back her head to laugh with genuine amusement at some of the funny things he was telling her. Women adored Max, that much was clear.

Miles smiled at her. 'You make a radiant bride, Alexi,' he told her. 'And I reckon you've got a good husband in Max Channing. I'd say he adores you, and that he's a man you can trust.'

Alexi nodded and her gaze swung back to her husband to find that he was watching her. There was a strange expression on his face, coolly thoughtful. It was hard to tell what was going on behind those blue eyes, but it was as if he was weighing her up, as if he was assessing her in some hard, calculating way. The thought made a shiver of apprehension race through her. Then he smiled and the coldness melted to warmth again, making her wonder if she was imagining things.

'I think we should leave now, Alexandra,' he said crisply. 'I want to be at the vineyard before nightfall.'

They all stood up as Alexi nodded, and goodbyes were said outside the restaurant. She felt strangely sad as she hugged Nancy and Miles and then climbed into the limousine with Max. It was as if things would never again be the same. Now that she was Mrs Channing a whole new life had begun and she wasn't entirely sure of what lay ahead.

They flew into the Napa Valley in Max's private jet. He had a landing-strip at the vineyard so it was simply a case of getting off the plane and taking a short jeep ride up to the house.

The sun was setting as Max pulled to a halt outside the steps to the main front door. A dusky pink haze lit the green of the countryside around them and reflected off the white walls of the impressive house. The air was

still and fragrant with the scent of jasmine and bou-
gainvillaea that covered the wrought-iron balustrade
around the veranda.

'This place is beautiful,' Alexi murmured as her eyes
moved over the large house. It had the style of a Spanish
villa, circled by white arches along the veranda which
ran along both the ground floor and the upper floor.
Large picture windows looked out across the garden and
then over the vineyards that seemed to stretch for miles
up towards the rolling green mountains.

'It's not bad,' Max conceded as he took her bag out
from the back of the car. 'I have a manager who runs
it for me and it ticks along quite well without my having
to come out too often.'

The door opened as they walked up the steps towards
it, and a young girl came out. Alexi judged her to be
about twenty-one or -two. Blonde and slender, she was
extremely attractive in a white miniskirt and short
cropped top.

'Max, how wonderful to see you again.' Her lips
curved in a wide smile and the bright eyes danced with
happiness.

'It's nice to see you too, Jo.' Max put down the bags
and reached a hand out to shake hers. 'Alexandra, this
is Joanne Bradley. She's the daughter of my manager
out here and she takes care of the house for me.'

'Pleased to meet you, Jo.' Alexi smiled in a friendly
fashion at the girl. Her smile met with a rather rude
stare as Joanne studied her, from her high-heeled shoes,
then over the champagne silk dress to the gleaming long
dark hair. Then she gave a curt nod and turned to lead
the way back into the house.

'I've started to prepare your favourite roast beef
dinner, Max,' she chatted to her boss as they entered the
wide entrance hall with a magnificent sweeping staircase.

Max laughed. 'I've already eaten quite a lot today, Jo.'

'Oh, I know you'll manage to eat my dinner, Max,' the girl said with confidence as she continued to lead the way upstairs and along the corridors. 'For afters I made you a special apple pie, just the way you like it.'

Max laughed again. 'You spoil me, Jo; it's no wonder I like to keep you around here.'

The girl opened up a door and they entered a most magnificent bedroom. A large four-poster bed covered in white and gold silk covers dominated the room. Chinese rugs covered the highly polished wood floors and a magnificent floral arrangement scented the room.

'As usual, the place looks superb.' Max put the luggage down and turned to smile at the girl.

'Thanks, Max,' she said cheerfully. 'Dad said he'll be over to see you in the morning.' She walked towards the door and then turned. 'How about dinner; should I turn it on?'

Max laughed and shook his head. 'I really couldn't eat anything else.' He turned an enquiring look at Alexi and she shook her head in agreement. She couldn't have faced another meal.

'Give us time to unpack and settle in and we will come down and have coffee a little later.'

The girl nodded and left them. The room was quiet after her bright chatter. Alexi searched around in her head for something to break that silence, a silence that had lain between them for virtually the whole of their trip here.

Max was busy unpacking his case. He looked deep in thought, a frown marring the smooth line of his forehead. He glanced over at her and caught her eye. 'The bathroom is through there if you want to take a shower.' He inclined his head towards the *en-suite* bathroom, then turned his attention back to unpacking.

'Thank you.' Alexi moved to open her case and took out a change of clothing, then she went into the bathroom and closed the door. For a moment she leaned back against it, her heart pounding. She felt so tense and on edge and, strangely, a little jealous of Joanne Bradley.

It was completely illogical; after all, she was married to Max. He had chosen her over all other women, and yet she couldn't shake the awful feeling. The feeling that she wasn't as important to him as he was to her. That there were a number of beautiful women in his life— women like Joanne who adored him, women who knew him so much better than she did. Women who knew what his favourite meal was, what he liked for breakfast…how to please him in bed.

She shook her head to dispel the ridiculous thoughts. What on earth had got in to her? she wondered furiously as she stepped across to switch on the shower. She was thinking like some immature schoolgirl.

She felt a lot better after standing under the full force of the shower jet. Then she dressed in a black skirt and a white lacy top and went back out to the bedroom.

Max was sitting at a bureau next to the window, leafing through some papers in front of him. He had already changed into a lightweight pair of trousers and a pale blue shirt. He looked casual and relaxed, yet there was nothing casual about the look in his eyes as she walked into the room.

'Have you got a moment, Alexandra?'

She moved to stand next to him. 'Yes, what is it?' Her eyes moved over the rugged features, the dark gleam of his hair, and she was filled with an overwhelming urge to run her fingers through it, to tell him to leave the paperwork in front of him and just take her in his arms.

'I just want you to sign this before we go downstairs.' He pushed the documents towards her and held out the pen for her to take.

'What is it?' She frowned as she pulled the papers closer to read.

'It's a marriage contract. It just states in black and white what will happen in the event of our divorce.' His voice was completely matter-of-fact, yet with every word he spoke Alexi could feel her whole body growing cold with shock and distaste.

'Divorce?' Her eyes were wide with disbelief as they turned towards him. 'We've only just got married, Max.'

He smiled; it was the kind of indulgent smile that an adult would give a child when she had said something completely naïve. 'I know, honey... it's just a safety net in case anything should go wrong in the future. It states exactly how much money and which of my properties you would receive in the event of our marriage breaking up.'

As she continued to stare at him incredulously, he tapped the end of the paper with the pen. 'Come along, honey. It's just as much for your benefit as mine.'

'You don't trust me, do you?' Her voice trembled slightly with the wealth of hurt that was welling up inside her.

'Of course I trust you.' He smiled. 'If I didn't I would have got you to sign this before I married you, not afterwards.' One eyebrow lifted as he gave her a quizzical look. 'Wouldn't I?'

She swallowed hard; she was desperately trying to get a grip of her wayward emotions. For an awful second she had felt as if she was going to cry.

'Perhaps you are the one who doesn't trust me?' he enquired now, and his voice took on a harder tone. 'I can assure you that the provisions for you in this con-

tract are more than generous. Perhaps you would like
to read over it thoroughly before signing?'

Alexi shook her head; she couldn't have given a damn
what provisions were made for her. She didn't want his
money... She couldn't have cared less about it. It was
his love that she wanted. She took the pen from his hand
and with a sweeping, decisive stroke signed her name to
where he had indicated.

'And here.' Calmly he turned the page and waited
while she signed that as well. 'Thank you.' He took back
the pen and then slipped the documents into the top
drawer of the bureau and locked it.

'There, that wasn't so bad, was it?' he enquired
smoothly. 'We can get on with our lives now and just
forget it.'

Alexi didn't think she would ever forget it. The green
eyes that watched him were filled with hurt.

He stood up and looked down at her pale face. 'Come
on, Alexandra, don't look like that. I was looking after
your interests as well as my own.'

She didn't say anything and he placed a hand under
her chin to tip her face up towards his. 'Don't you trust
me... hmm?' The deep voice was silky-smooth and it
sent shivers racing down her spine.

His question met with silence. She loved Max but she
couldn't say that she completely trusted him. The dis-
covery shocked her; how could you marry somebody
when you didn't entirely trust them?

'Alexandra?' His voice coaxed for an answer and when
she still didn't give one his lips twisted in a grim smile.
'I see...'

'Well, what do you expect when you force me to sign
that kind of contract, Max? It's so cold-
blooded...especially on our wedding night,' she murmured softly.

'I didn't force you, Alexandra.'

'But then again you didn't leave me with much choice, did you?' Her voice was scornful as anger started to take the place of pain.

'Of course you had a choice. There is always a choice.' There was a note of impatience in the brisk tone now.

'And I think I made the wrong one when I married you,' she flared suddenly, her temper and her emotions just taking over. 'Right at this moment I don't think I even like you.' She didn't mean the words—even as she said them she knew that she didn't mean them—but there was something inside that just wanted to strike out at him. She wanted to hurt him the way he had hurt her. She would have swung away from him at that point but he caught hold of her arm in a painful grip and swung her firmly to face him.

'You don't like me very much?' He grated the words scornfully. 'Why is that, Alexandra? Is it because you had designs on my wealth? Did you marry me because the alimony would be juicy?'

'Don't be ridiculous. You're forgetting that my father is a very wealthy man, and I am a successful business-woman. I don't need anything from you.' She tried to extricate herself from his grip without any success. 'You're hurting me.' She looked up at him accusingly.

'Really.' He sounded completely unconcerned and he made no attempt to release her. 'I'm not forgetting any-thing...especially who your father is. Believe me, Alexandra, every time I look at you I'm reminded who your father is. You're just as arrogant, just as materi-alistic and stubborn.'

Her face flared a bright, angry red. 'How dare you talk about my father like that?'

His lips twisted in a hard line. 'I was actually talking mostly about you. I could say a lot worse about your father.' As he spoke, his hand released her arm and moved to the buttons on her blouse. Slowly he unfastened the top one then moved to the next.

She trembled as his fingers touched her skin. 'What do you think you are doing?' The anger in her tone was tinged with apprehension now.

'I'm putting an end to the discussion; I'm growing bored with it.' Calmly he continued to work his way down the row of buttons until the top hung open exposing the white lacy bra underneath.

For a moment she stood absolutely still, shock and nerves holding her rigid.

Then his fingers moved to the front fastening on the bra and her hand flew to push him away. 'Stop it, Max,' she breathed furiously.

A spark of amusement lit his eyes now and one eyebrow lifted. 'Now who's being cold-blooded?' His hand firmly moved hers away and went back to the front fastener.

'I said, stop it.' She was furiously angry now as she moved again to push his hand away.

'Does this mean you don't want me to make love to you?' He sounded more lazily amused than annoyed.

'It means I don't want you to come anywhere near me,' she retorted sharply.

'Don't tell me I've got myself a frigid wife,' he jeered softly.

Without stopping to think about it, her hand swung back and she lashed out furiously, catching him a stinging blow to the side of his face.

The blue eyes darkened with anger and suddenly Alexi's temper evaporated, leaving remorse and more than a little fear in its place. Her hand dropped to her side and she stared up at him, waiting with a kind of hushed breathlessness to see how he was going to react.

'That wasn't very clever, Alexandra,' he drawled, and there was an ominous sound to his voice that made her very uneasy. 'I think that spoilt Ms Rossini needs to be taught a lesson.'

She took a step back from him, her heart pounding with apprehension. 'It's Mrs Channing now, remember?' She tried to force herself to sound flippant and unafraid, but her voice wasn't entirely steady. She tipped her head up defiantly and made herself meet his gaze with a look of arrogant bravery that warned him to back off or else...

For a moment he smiled as if he found her genuinely amusing. Then he stepped forward until he was nearly touching her. 'Then I think you need a lesson on how Mrs Channing should act,' he drawled huskily. His hand reached to cup her chin and his mouth claimed hers in a kiss that was so sensual that it sent tingles of pleasure rippling through her.

Immediately she forgot the angry exchange that had gone before. Her mind and her body were totally absorbed in his kiss. Her hands moved up over the smooth material of his shirt to rest on his shoulders, loving the feeling of heat that emanated through the fine clothing.

His head lifted and his lips gave a half-smile at her complete submission. His eyes held hers as his hand returned to the fastener of her bra. This time she allowed him to undo it, then he started to slip her blouse down her arms, making her drop her hands from his shoulders. Both items of clothing dropped to the floor. Then his hands covered the soft roundness of her bare breasts. Her eyes flickered closed at the sweet ecstasy of the caress as he softly stroked her. Then his hands were moving to the zip of her skirt; it slid easily to join the other clothing on the floor.

All she wore now was a very flimsy pair of lacy panties. As his hand lingered over them her eyes flew open to drown in the blueness of his gaze. He smiled, an almost triumphant smile, and the panties were removed with a smooth stroke of his hands as he ran them down over her hips.

Instead of taking her in his arms as she expected him to do at that point, he stepped back and his eyes very calmly moved over her naked body.

'Very beautiful,' he murmured lazily. 'Now say, "Please, Max, make love to me."'

Her eyes clouded, puzzled by his behaviour.

He smiled and his hand touched her breast again. 'I don't want you saying that I forced you into anything,' he drawled, a hint of amusement in the husky tone. 'So repeat after me... "Please, Max..."'

The deep blue eyes watched her lips. She remained silent, her pride warring with the strong desire flooding through her.

He smiled then lowered his lips towards hers in a kiss that was so intensely passionate that it literally made her go weak at the knees.

'Well?' He lifted his lips fractionally to huskily murmur the question.

She curled her fingers through the short darkness of his hair. 'Please, Max.' Her voice was a mere whisper in the silence of the room as pride gave way to the stronger emotions inside her.

As soon as she had spoken, he swept her up into his arms and carried her to the bed.

When Alexandra woke the next morning she was alone in the large double bed. Sunlight flooded through the window, bathing the gold and white covers over her and lighting the room with a brilliance that made her blink. She stretched, feeling lethargically comfortable swathed in the softness of silk sheets. Memories of the night before returned with a vivid rush and she turned her head towards the pillow beside her, wondering where her husband was.

She sat up, pushing her long hair back out of her eyes as she searched the room. It was silent and empty; obviously Max had gone downstairs. She felt strangely alone, which was weird because she woke every morning on her own. But she couldn't help wishing that Max was here, then maybe he would have kissed her good morning tenderly and told her he loved her.

Her eyes clouded for a moment. Their night together had been beautiful. Tender and passionate, Max was all she could ever have dreamed of in a lover and then more. But he still hadn't made any declarations of love and that fact had made Alexi remain silent. She had hidden the depth of her feelings for him behind the sweetness of her kiss. Then there was that contract that he had asked her to sign... Just thinking about it again made her unbearably sad.

With a sigh she got up out of bed. They had only a couple of days here on honeymoon; she was going to try to put everything out of her mind and just relax.

She showered and then put on a pale yellow sun-dress. It was shorter than she normally wore, and she stopped to examine her appearance in the full-length mirror before leaving the room. Her long legs were already lightly bronzed from the Californian sun; her figure was slender yet curved in all the right places. Even though her appearance was pleasing to the eye she still felt slightly nervous as she went in search of Max.

She admired the house once again as she walked back through it. Obviously no expense had been spared on the décor, yet it was tastefully done. Not too ostentatious, it was comfortably stylish.

The living-room was empty and the only sound came from what Alexi presumed to be the kitchen. She could hear men's voices and the rattle of dishes. Presuming that Joanne was preparing breakfast for Max, she took a deep breath and went to join them.

Apart from Joanne the kitchen was empty. The sound of men's voices came from the lively chatter of a radio programme.

'Good morning.' Alexi smiled brightly at the girl as she looked up from her baking.

'More like afternoon,' Joanne said in a rather sullen tone as she pointedly looked at the brass clock on the wall behind her.

'Is it?' Alexi followed her gaze and saw to her surprise that it was nearly ten o'clock, hardly the afternoon, but much later than she would normally have got up.

'There's coffee in the pot if you want it.' Joanne made no attempt to leave what she was doing to get it for her. Not that Alexi minded; she didn't want to put the girl out in any way, but she did resent her hostile attitude.

'Thank you.' Calmly she walked to the pot and poured herself a cup of the steaming liquid. 'Have you seen Max this morning?' she asked casually.

'Yes, we had breakfast together at eight,' Joanne replied without looking up from her work. She was measuring out flour on a set of brass scales and adding it to the mixing-bowl in front of her.

'I see.' Alexi wished the girl hadn't made breakfast sound quite so intimate; it made a shiver of irritation flick through her. 'And did he say where he was going afterwards?'

'The vineyard.' The answer was curt, as if Alexi was asking for classified information. Then there was silence.

For a moment Alexi watched the other girl contemplatively. She was dressed in a tight pair of faded denim jeans that clung to her slender figure in a most provocative way. Her top was a cropped T-shirt in a bright cherry-red. It was casual attire, yet it looked very sexy. She found herself wondering if Max had thought the same thing when he had sat opposite her at breakfast.

'Max told me that you married him yesterday.'

The sudden abrupt statement startled Alexi a little. Then she had to smile at the way Joanne somehow made their wedding sound one-sided. 'Yes, we were married yesterday,' she said with a nod.

'It surprised me.' The girl poured the remaining flour into the bowl and started to mix it with brisk efficiency.

'Why?' she tried very hard not to sound as on edge as she felt.

'Because he's in love with another woman, that's why.' The girl imparted the information quite calmly without even looking up. 'Her name is Carole and he has brought her here on several occasions.'

There was a stunned silence. Somehow at the back of her mind Alexi had been preparing herself to hear that Joanne had had an affair with Max, but to hear that he was in love with someone else completely floored her.

Unfortunately at that moment Max came into the kitchen accompanied by another man.

'Good morning.' His gaze lingered on Alexi's face and then moved to take in the rest of her appearance, a gleam of male appreciation in his eyes. 'Tony, I'd like you to meet my wife, Alexandra.'

From somewhere Alexi got the strength to be able to smile politely at the older man, even though her mind was racing wildly in all kinds of crazy directions.

'Tony is Jo's father and my very efficient manager here,' Max went on to explain.

'Well, I try,' Tony said with a good-natured grin. Then to Alexi's surprise he leaned across and kissed her cheek. 'I wish you all the happiness in the world, young lady. It's about time someone clipped this fella's wings and made him settle down.'

Max laughed with genuine amusement at that. 'Now what makes you think she's clipped my wings, Tony? She's merely shortened them a fraction, that's all.'

The words were said with light-hearted humour, but they somehow managed to make Alexi feel even more unhappy.

Meanwhile Jo was fussing around the kitchen, pouring the men coffee and setting cakes out for them at the table.

'So what kind of season are we having so far?' Max asked his manager conversationally as they moved to sit down.

'Dry.' Tony Bradley laughed. 'We're issuing the same old slogan again this year. "Save water, drink wine".'

Max smiled. 'And indeed I think people are taking the advice. Our turnover is most definitely increasing.'

The men became immersed in a conversation about the business which Alexi listened to with only half her attention, the other part of her was thinking about Joanne's words. Was it true? Was Max in love with another woman? If so, why hadn't he married her? The questions raced around and around until she felt as if her head would split.

In the end she put her cup down on the counter and excused herself from the room, saying she needed some fresh air. They glanced up at her and Max's eyes were sharp for a moment as they rested on her pale countenance, then he merely nodded and resumed his conversation.

The air outside was anything but fresh. After the coolness of the air-conditioning, the heat hit her like a molten wave. It shimmered over the rows of vines stretching out towards the horizon. Alexi walked down through the garden to the gate that led out to the vineyard, and for a moment she leaned against it as her eyes took in the beauty of her surrounding.

The air was still and silent except for the sound of water as the sprays irrigated the ground. It was a surprise therefore when Max's voice spoke right next to her. Her head whirled around as he came to stand beside her.

He smiled, that lop-sided smile that was just too damned attractive. 'Everything all right, Alexandra?'

'Of course.' Her eyes moved back to the view in front of her. 'Why shouldn't it be?' Even to her own ears her voice sounded surly.

'No reason. I just thought you were very quiet back in there. Sorry I had to leave you this morning, but I did have a bit of business to get through while I was here.' His voice was calmly matter-of-fact, as if he were speaking to some stranger, she thought heatedly.

'That's perfectly all right, Max, I do understand that business must come first. You made that very clear when you announced that you were cutting our honeymoon short.' Her voice was cool, which was strange considering the heat building up inside her. He made her so angry. The whole situation was making her damned angry what with last night's fiasco of the contract and now hearing about this other woman.

There was silence for a moment. 'I'm afraid that my attention to business is something you will have to get used to, Alexandra,' he said impassively.

Her lips tightened angrily. 'Just as I will have to get used to you seeing other women?' The question somehow slipped out although she had never intended to ask it.

'I beg your pardon?' His tone held an ominous note; there was certainly nothing apologetic about it.

She took a deep breath and then forced herself to swing around and face him. She would have to ask him . . . She couldn't keep the question bottled inside for any length of time; it would send her crazy. 'Who is Carole?'

'Carole?' His face showed no kind of emotion.

'Carole, the woman you have brought here several times,' she enlightened him further, her voice barely containing her impatience and anger.

One eyebrow lifted in that quizzical look of his and his mouth twisted slightly. Whether he was angry or just amused, Alexi couldn't tell. 'Carole Burns,' he told her in a dry tone.

When he made no attempt to enlighten her further, Alexi's hands balled into fists at her sides. 'And who is she?' Hell, the man would make a good poker player, she thought grimly; it was nigh on impossible to get anything out of him.

'She's a business acquaintance, although what it has to do with you I don't know,' he said with a shake of his head.

'Considering I am your wife, I think I have every right to know who you are having affairs with,' she told him through clenched teeth.

Much to her fury he threw back his head and laughed at that with genuine amusement. 'We were only married yesterday, Alexandra . . . I have hardly had time to cheat on you yet.'

Alexi didn't like to be laughed at and she didn't like the yet that he tagged on the end of that statement. Rage sizzled through her and she made to turn away from him before she really let go and said something she would regret.

However Max had other ideas and he wasn't about to let her march away. He caught hold of her arm and held her where she was. 'I suppose I have Joanne to thank for this outburst?' he asked, a note of displeasure in the firm voice.

She frowned. 'It is not an outburst; I am simply asking a question.'

'I know what you are asking,' he stated in an arid voice. 'And the answer is no. No, I am not having an affair with Carole. She is the wife of one of my most valued friends.'

'Oh.' Alexi glanced up at him uncertainly. The dark face was seriously intent. All of a sudden she felt incredibly foolish to have made such a fuss over some woman she had never even seen.

'Oh, indeed,' he said in a droll tone. 'Were you by any chance jealous, Alexandra?'

'Don't be ridiculous,' she said briskly. 'I was simply curious.'

He reached out a hand and tilted her head up so she was forced to meet his eyes. 'And you know what curiosity did, don't you?' he drawled. 'Curiosity can be a very dangerous thing.'

Alexi didn't like the tone to his voice; it was as if he was warning her off. He bent his head and his lips found hers in a long, hard kiss. But despite the warmth of that kiss there was a chill that raced right through her. Something was wrong... Something was terribly wrong.

CHAPTER SEVEN

'I KNOW it's probably a selfish statement, but I'm glad you weren't away for any longer than a few days, Alexi,' Miles murmured as they went through the accounts together at the end of her second week back. 'It's amazing how the work piles up when you are short-staffed.'

'It certainly is.' Alexi smiled. 'I could do with another few days off to recuperate from the havoc my holiday created in my workload.'

Miles grinned. 'Hinting around a second honeymoon already...? Must be love.'

'Maybe,' Alexi answered non-committally as she busied herself leafing through the papers on her desk.

'No maybe about it,' he said laughing. 'You returned to this office starry-eyed. Even the papers are talking about "the romance of the year".'

'I wonder how they managed to know about our wedding?' Alexi frowned as she thought about the Georgia Gold column. It had been a shock to lift the papers this morning and read about herself and Max.

'Beats me how that woman seems to know about everything,' Miles said with a shake of his head. 'I think she missed her way; she should be working for the FBI. At least she managed to get all the facts straight this time.'

'I just wish I could have got in contact with my father before the papers caught hold of the story. Now it seems everyone in Hollywood knows I'm married except him,' Alexi said sadly.

'Well, you did try your best to reach him, honey. It's not your fault that he didn't return your calls,' Miles said firmly, then changed the subject. 'Nancy wants to know if you and Max will come to dinner next week?'

'Max is still in New York,' Alexi said with a frown.

'Won't he be back next week?'

There was silence for a moment. 'I don't know, Miles,' she admitted slowly. 'Like my father, he hasn't been in contact with me since he left. Those two seem to have a lot in common.' The words were spoken in a light tone, but the eyes she lifted towards her friend were filled with anxiety.

'Max is a very busy man, Alexi; he runs several successful businesses scattered all over the world. I should think his time is very rarely his own.'

She nodded and looked back down at the papers in front of her. She understood that he was a busy man, but it only took a few minutes to lift the phone. Where was he now? Who was he with? Once more the questions returned to plague her.

She had been pleased to be kept so busy this week. At least her every waking thought hadn't been about her husband. It was different when she returned to his house in the evening. There she was in his domain; she slept alone in his bed at night and she was tormented by thoughts of him.

She missed him more than she had imagined possible. She missed the way he held her in his arms at night. She missed the lop-sided smile when she had amused him, the warmth of his blue eyes.

For a moment her mind returned to their time together in the Napa Valley. Despite the stormy start to their honeymoon she had enjoyed her time with him and had been sorry to leave the tranquil beauty of the vineyard. Even Joanne had been quite pleasant to her after her outburst in the kitchen. Alexi had secretly wondered if

Max had had a word with the girl to make her behave in a more civil manner. Just thinking about that incident made her mind return to the mysterious Carole. The woman's name had not been mentioned again, but that hadn't stopped Alexi wondering.

'Alexi?' Miles's voice interrupted her train of thought. 'Alexi, you haven't heard a word I've just said, have you?'

'Sorry, Miles, I was daydreaming.'

He laughed at that. 'I can guess who about. Why don't you finish early today, Alexi? You've worked hard this week; you deserve an afternoon off.'

Alexi thought about it for a moment. 'I don't know, Miles——'

They were interrupted by Alexi's secretary speaking through the intercom. 'I have your father on the line for you, Alexi,' she said.

Alexi lifted startled eyes towards Miles.

'I'll leave you alone so you can talk,' he said with a grin and headed for the door.

She reached for the phone. 'Hello, Henri,' she said as she leaned back against the soft leather of her chair.

'What the hell are you playing at?'

Instead of the dulcet tone she had expected, her father sounded furiously angry. He didn't give her a chance to respond before continuing abruptly. 'Is it true that you've married Maxwell Channing?'

'It's true,' she answered steadily. Then as there was an ominous silence from the other end of the line she hurriedly continued, 'I'm sorry I didn't get to tell you the news earlier. I have been trying to get in touch with you for a while; I desperately wanted you to be here for the wedding.'

Still silence. 'Henri, are you still there?' she ventured gently.

'Just about,' he answered grimly. 'Hell, woman, what made you do such a damn fool thing?'

The question made her lips curve. 'I'm in love with him, Dad.'

There was a muffled curse at the other end of the line. 'You do realise that you have just made the worst mistake of your life?' he bit out roughly.

'I don't think so, Henri,' she said with quiet dignity. She had more or less been expecting her father's disapproval. He never had a good word to say about any of her boyfriends; he usually thought that they weren't good enough for her. To find out that she had married so quickly must have come as a shock.

'I damn well know so.' His voice was abrasive. 'The man is an out and out rogue. You don't think that a man like Channing married you because he loved you…do you?' Henri Rossini didn't believe in the gentle approach; his voice dripped scorn. 'I'm taking the first plane home to sort this out.'

'Henri——' The line went dead, cutting her off with a sharp click as Henri Rossini banged the receiver down.

For a long while she just sat staring at the phone, then she gathered her things together and left the office.

It probably was a bad idea to leave work, but she couldn't possibly have concentrated on anything after that conversation. She found it hard enough keeping her mind on her driving as she took the coast road out to Malibu, her father's words echoing and re-echoing through her head. 'You don't think a man like Channing married you because he loved you?'

Determinedly she tried to push the words away. Henri would disapprove of her marriage no matter whom it was with, she told herself sternly. Yet the fear inside her continued to grow. Henri had sounded so positive that she had made a mistake, had sounded as if he knew Max Channing better than she did. That wouldn't be hard, a little voice whispered inside, because she hardly knew her husband at all.

Henri Rossini arrived back late the following night. The phone rang shrilly at the house at about eleven and Alexi thought it would be her father as she picked it up; she had long since given up hoping that Max would call her. It was Monica. 'Your father wants you to come up to the house right away,' she said in a clipped tone, then replaced the receiver.

Alexi pursed her lips angrily. It was like being given a royal summons...typical of her father's behaviour. But Monica could at least have been a little more pleasant...could have wished her well in her marriage or said something polite.

Alexi seethed quietly inside and for a while she contemplated ignoring the call, but that would only incense her father further and she had no wish to do that. Also she was intensely curious to know what he had to say to her.

It was the early hours of the morning when Alexi stopped the Lamborghini outside the gates to her father's house. The security guard swung the light over her and the large electric gates swung open to admit her. She drove up the long winding drive with haste and parked at the bottom of the steps leading up to the mansion.

Monica opened the door to her. She was wearing a long black dress that fitted to every curve of her body like a second skin, her blonde hair was sitting neatly in place, and her face was like a cool mask of displeasure. 'What took you so long?' she demanded as she stood back and allowed her to enter.

'I got here as quickly as possible.' Alexi restrained her temper with difficulty. She had never really liked her father's girlfriend, but her manner was particularly objectionable tonight. She couldn't help thinking that if

Max had been with her the woman would have been decidedly more pleasant.

'I believe you are living with Max now,' Monica said over her shoulder as she led the way across the vast white marble entrance hall towards one of the many doors on the far side.

'We were married a fortnight ago,' Alexi answered tersely. Monica obviously knew she was married . . . the whole of California knew about it since Georgia Gold's column.

Monica said nothing. She opened the double doors that led into a sumptuous lounge, and stood back to let Alexi pass her. 'Your daughter is here for you, darling,' she said huskily and then closed the door to leave the two of them alone, something that surprised Alexi. Obviously she had been told by Henri that her presence was not required; maybe that was why she was being so damn rude.

Henri was standing by the Adam fireplace, his back towards her, his hands stretched out towards the roaring flames of the fire. He was dressed immaculately as always in a dark grey suit that was hand-tailored and fitted his powerful frame to perfection. 'So, you little fool, you've really made a mess of things this time,' he breathed in a low, angry tone without turning even to look at her.

She swallowed hard, hurt beyond reason that he didn't turn and take her in his arms. She knew he was furious with her, but he could have greeted her before launching in for the attack. 'Hello, Henri,' she murmured. 'Welcome home.'

'Welcome home?' His voice was so heavy with scorn that it grated and almost broke. Then he turned to face her.

Alexi was shocked when she saw his face. Henri Rossini was a good-looking man; his hair was thick, the darkness streaked with silver, and his face was remarkably young-looking for his sixty years. But tonight he looked grey in his face, his mouth in a bitter line, his dark eyes haunted with rage. 'You'll have to leave him, Alexi; we can get the marriage annulled and forget it has ever taken place.' The words were issued like a demand and for a moment she could only stare at him in bewilderment.

'Why?' she asked in a cracked voice.

'Because Channing has married you for one reason only.' Henri paused for a moment before continuing in a strangely low tone. 'He married you for revenge.'

At first Alexi thought she had misheard him. She frowned, completely at a loss. 'Revenge? Henri, I don't understand you. What possible reason would Max have to hate me that much?' She almost felt like laughing with relief as she asked the question. The idea was too ludicrous to have any truth in it.

'He hates you because you are my daughter.' Henri growled the words. 'He'd like to destroy me the way I destroyed his father twenty-three years ago.'

'Twenty-three years ago?' Alexi's eyebrows lifted, and she wondered suddenly if her father was going a little crazy. 'What on earth are you talking about, Henri? Max would have been a mere boy all those years ago. I certainly don't think——'

'You don't know what you're talking about.' Henri cut across her impatiently. 'Max may have been young, but he was old enough to remember what I did to his father.' Henri fell silent and his eyes held a far-away look as if he was going back into the past. Alexi didn't dare to speak; she could only hold her breath and wait for him to explain.

'Your mother left me for Edward Channing.' The words exploded into the silence of the room. He nodded as he saw the shocked expression on her face. 'Yes, she left me for Max's father. Took you when you were only six months old and moved in with him.' His voice was biting hard, his eyes alive with tormented memories. 'I told her that it was a situation I would not tolerate... I warned her what would happen, but she didn't take me seriously enough... She underestimated my power in this town.'

'What did you do?' Alexi's voice was a hoarse whisper; she hardly dared ask the question, yet she had to know... had to know all the awful details.

'I ruined him, it was as simple as that. She was only with him for a couple of months and in that time I made sure that first he lost his business, then his house. Eleanor had no other choice but to leave him after that. She moved into a rented house; Edward Channing went back to England.'

Alexi swallowed hard, shocked beyond words at her father's brutality. 'How could you do that?' she whispered. 'How could you?'

'My dear girl, nobody makes a fool of Henri Rossini and gets away with it,' he grated scornfully. 'Just as Max Channing thinks he has made a fool of me now by marrying you...' Henri shook his head. 'He has miscalculated for once in his life.'

Alexi shook her head. 'I don't believe that's why Max married me. He would have no real gain from doing something like that, and anyway, he's not that kind of a man.'

'If you think that then I'd say you don't know Channing at all; believe me, he is very much that kind of man.'

There was silence for a moment as Henri watched the different expressions crossing his daughter's face. Disbelief, fear... sadness, they were all there.

She remembered Max telling her about the woman who had moved in to his father's house for a short period of time as a kind of housekeeper, a woman with a small baby... She had had no idea that woman had been her mother.

'There was nothing between my mother and Max's father,' she whispered softly almost to herself. 'She didn't leave you for him. She left because she was unbearably unhappy.' Alexi fell silent for a moment before continuing in an incredulous tone. 'She never even mentioned the name Channing to me—but then I was much too young to understand about something that had all happened when I was just a baby. She did tell me that she had always loved you, Henri, and that there had never been another man.'

Henri's face seemed to go ashen at that statement. 'Go home Alexi.' His voice was strained as he completely ignored her words. 'Go back to your own house and let me take care of things. We can have the marriage annulled in next to no time.'

She shook her head. She couldn't leave Max; the very thought made her want to break down and weep. 'I can't,' she murmured brokenly, 'and anyway I can't go home. I've sold my house; the contracts were signed a couple of days ago.'

'You've what?' The tense voice exploded into anger. 'Who have you sold to?'

Alexi shrugged. 'I don't know—some big company. They've been after it for ages. They paid a very good price for it.'

'I'm sure they did,' her father said drily. 'I'm also willing to bet that you sold to Holland Enterprises. They bought the land just behind it... beat me to it, destroying my plans to develop the place.'

'I don't know.' She shrugged. 'It doesn't matter, Henri. I needed an extra cash injection for my business; it's been going through a difficult time and——'

'And I bet Max said, "Sell the house, Alexi, you don't need it",' her father cut across her drily.

She nodded reluctantly, her heart sinking as Henri continued, 'That's because he owns Holland Enterprises and he stands to make a couple of million once that land is turned into a golfing and leisure complex.'

Alexi's skin turned a porcelain-white. She felt almost sick for a moment as she leaned against the side of a chair.

'What a conquest Channing has made. He must be congratulating himself right at this moment. Not only has he succeeded in taking Henri Rossini's daughter, he's made a million on the deal as well,' Henri finished grimly.

Alexi couldn't say anything. Her insides were churning.

'You'd better sit down,' Henri said with a twist of his lips as he observed how upset she was.

She did as she was told and he walked to the drinks cabinet to pour her a brandy. 'I'll sort it out,' he said grimly as he crossed and pressed the glass into her shaking hand. 'Meanwhile you had better stay here.'

She felt a little better after the fiery liquid had warmed the ice-cold feeling inside. 'Maybe I will stay, but just for tonight.' She was in no fit state to drive back to Malibu now and she knew it.

'You'll stay longer than that. It will take time to sort out somewhere decent for you to live and——'

'I don't know, Henri.' She cut across him.

'You don't know what?' he demanded harshly. 'You're surely not contemplating staying with that man? You couldn't be that stupid? The man has married you because you are a Rossini, because he stood to make a lot of money... There is no sentiment involved, believe me.'

'Stop it, Henri...stop it.' Her voice rose in fury at the words she didn't want to hear. 'I don't know what I'm going to do, but you'll have to leave me to deal with it in my own way.'

'I don't think so, Alexi,' he rasped harshly. 'I think you've made enough of a mess as it is. We will have to be very careful how we handle this. I don't want the newspapers getting hold of the story; we will be a laughing-stock.'

Alexi shot him a look of anguish. 'Quite frankly, Henri, how I look in the newspapers is the least of my worries.'

'Maybe that is of no consequence to you, my girl,' he said furiously. 'But I have a lot of business deals in the pipelines. A story like this could ruin my credibility.'

'You mean it could ruin your reputation as "Mr Nice Guy" if word gets out about how you treated Edward Channing,' she murmured bitterly.

'I mean that I don't want this story to break in any circumstances. I avoided the glare of the Press last time and I am determined to do it again. I will not have your mother's name dragged through the scandal columns... Have I made myself clear?'

There was no arguing with Henri Rossini when he spoke in that tone. Alexi nodded, suddenly feeling tired. 'Yes, Father, you've made everything crystal-clear.' She rose to her feet. 'If you'll excuse me I'll go up to bed.'

He smiled, relaxing now that he thought she would do as she was told. 'You can have your old room back,' he told her. 'Welcome home, Alexi.'

'Welcome home, Alexi.' The words filtered through her tired brain as she lay alone in her bed and stared up at the ceiling. What was she going to do when Max came home? Did she have the strength to leave him? She tossed and turned and buried her head into her pillow to weep bitter tears. She loved Maxwell Channing... No matter what he had done and for what reason, she still loved him.

She awoke the following morning with a thumping headache. She had hardly slept all night; she had gone over and over her father's words, trying to discount them, trying to tell herself that there was no truth in

them. But it was no use; she would have to face the truth
sooner or later. The very fact that Max hadn't bothered
even to ring her while he was away told her clearly what
he felt about her.

She dressed and went downstairs to find her father.
He was having breakfast out on the terrace with Monica.
She had just been for a dip in the large swimming-pool
behind them and was wrapped in a huge towelling robe.

'Good morning.' Henri's sharp eyes raked over his
daughter's pale countenance. 'Have some coffee, Alexi,
and David will fetch you some breakfast.' He nodded
towards the member of staff standing by the open French
doors.

'No, I'm all right, thank you.' She shook her head.
'I'm going to head off now.'

'Off where?' Immediately there was a wary note to
her father's voice.

'Back to Malibu... It's all right, Dad.' She held up
her hand as her father looked set to interrupt. 'Max is
in New York.'

'I see.' Henri reached for the coffee-pot and poured
another cup. 'Stick around for a while, Alexi. Martin
will arrive any minute and I know he'd like to see you.'

'I thought Martin was in England?' Alexi frowned.

'He was, but he flew back with me. We don't need
him out there for a couple of weeks.'

'So you thought you'd bring him back to keep me
occupied while you sorted out the problem of Maxwell
Channing?' Alexi guessed with a bitter twist of her lips.

'Don't be ridiculous, girl.' Henri shot her a warning
glance that Monica was watching the proceedings with
avid interest.

'I have to go, Dad.' Alexi turned away.

'Collect your things and come straight back.' Her
father's voice followed her across the terrace as she
moved to leave.

'I don't know, Dad.' She waved her hand as she walked down the steps leading around to the car. 'I don't know what I'm going to do.'

It was a beautiful day; the sun was shining down from a clear blue sky that seemed to match the blue of the sea. If was too good a day to feel depressed, Alexi told herself as she put her foot down and sped along the coast road. But, try as she did, her spirits wouldn't lift.

When she turned into Max's driveway the first thing she saw was his car. Max was home. There was also another car that she didn't recognise sitting next to it. Either they had visitors or Max had bought yet another vehicle.

She climbed out into the warm morning air and stood looking up at the house for a moment. Her heart was thudding against her chest. What should she do? Should she confront him with all the accusations welling up inside? Or should she act as if nothing had happened and just play it all by ear?

The front door opened on to the balcony and Max stepped out into the sunlight. For a moment she allowed herself to feast her eyes on him. It was so long since she had seen him; two whole weeks seemed an eternity. He looked more handsome than ever. The dark hair gleamed in the sunlight, and the designer suit looked superb on the strong, athletic-type body.

'Where have you been?' His voice was a deep rasp, no welcoming smile, no, 'How have you been?' There were times when Max reminded her forcibly of her father.

'Out visiting.' She was loath to say straight out where she had been. She would pick her time to mention her father.

'Am I not allowed to know who with?' he enquired silkily.

'Do you mean to say you're interested? I thought as you hadn't rung since leaving that you weren't particularly bothered about what I was doing.'

'OK, maybe I deserve that,' he murmured.

There was silence while she just stood and stared up at him.

'Well, are you coming up here or not?' he enquired with a grin.

She hesitated for a moment and then walked up the steps. He watched her every movement, taking in the glossy fall of her dark hair and the cropped top she wore above the designer denim jeans. As she got to the top of the steps she lifted her head up and he smiled.

'You're looking good. A bit pale, perhaps.' His eyes lingered on the almost transparent hue of her skin.

'I didn't get much sleep last night.'

'I gathered that when I arrived at four this morning and found the bed empty,' he said drily. 'Were you with another man?'

'Would you care?' She flung the words at him contemptuously.

One dark eyebrow lifted. 'Of course I'd care. You are mine, Alexandra. Nobody has the right to touch you except me.' His voice was suddenly like steel. His hand reached out as he was talking and he pulled her into his arms in a none too gentle way to kiss her with a kind of fierce passion on her lips.

'So where were you?' he asked as he lifted his head.

'Where were you?' she threw the question back at him.

'You know where I was. I was in New York.'

'New York is a big place,' she answered tartly.

He grinned. 'I was staying at the Sheldon. I know I should have phoned, but I've been very busy.'

'I'm sure you have.' She brushed past him towards the side-door that led into the main corridor of the house.

She made straight for the bedroom, conscious that he was following her. When she got there she opened up the wardrobe and started to take out some of her clothes.

'Alexandra, we have...' Max stopped dead in the doorway. 'What the hell do you think you're doing?' he grated angrily as she took one of her cases out as well.

'What does it look like I'm doing?' she asked calmly while inside her heart was hammering wildly. 'I'm leaving.'

'Like hell you are.' He took the case from her nerveless fingers and flung it back into the wardrobe.

She swung to face him, her eyes blazing like emeralds. 'Don't pretend you give a damn.'

One eyebrow lifted. 'Do you want to tell me what this is all about?'

There was silence for a moment. 'I've seen my father and he has told me everything.'

If she had thought that would make him look worried she couldn't have been more wrong. His mouth curved in cynical amusement. 'Not everything!' he drawled in mock-horror.

Her lips tightened. At this moment she hated Maxwell Channing with a passion. How dared he poke fun at her...? How dared he sneer?

'Well, are you going to enlighten me further?' he continued.

'You don't need me to enlighten you,' she murmured bitterly. 'You know exactly what Henri told me.'

He shrugged. 'Not really. I could guess, I suppose. I presume that he is still the same bitter, twisted old man?'

'Don't speak about my father like that.' She flared to Henri's defence.

'I hope you rushed to vindicate me so loyally when Rossini stuck his knife in,' he said drily.

'He told me nothing more than the facts.' Alexi flushed uncomfortably.

'Did he, now?' Max drawled sardonically, then his tone changed to a hard, accusing one. 'Did he tell you how he systematically set out to ruin my father?'

'Yes.' She dropped her eyes from the accusation in his face for a moment before continuing. 'He also told me that you married me out of revenge . . . that you were only interested in getting back at him.'

'Did he, now?' Max made no attempt to deny the accusation. His hand reached out and he tipped her head up so that she was forced to look him straight in the eye. Then his hand slipped from her chin to the front button on her T-shirt.

'What the hell do you think you're doing?' She pushed him away with a forceful hand.

'Extracting some more revenge.' His voice was matter-of-fact, his lips curved in a half-smile that was vaguely mocking.

Her hand swung upwards to hit him across the face, only he was too quick for her and caught her arm in mid-air. 'We've been through that before,' he murmured. 'And if you remember it didn't do you very much good, did it?'

Her face flared a bright red at the vivid memory of just what had happened last time she had hit him. 'I hate you,' she told him through clenched teeth.

The amusement died from his face. 'Do you?' he drawled and pulled her roughly in towards him. 'How much do you hate me?' His lips ground down over hers in a punishing kiss.

She pushed against his chest, but to no avail; his grip only tightened and his lips crushed hers mercilessly.

The sudden shrill ring of the telephone made his hold relax, and she took the opportunity to pull away. Her breathing was coming in painful gasps and her heart was pounding like crazy in her chest. She stared at him with wide eyes, hating him, loving him. At that moment the two feelings were almost inseparable; she couldn't think straight at all.

The telephone stopped ringing as Rosie answered it in the kitchen. A few moments later she was tapping on the bedroom door. 'There is a Mr Steel on the line for Mrs Channing,' she called.

A jolt of surprise shot through Alexi. What on earth was Martin doing ringing her here?

Max's expression darkened ominously as his eyes met with hers. 'Well, well, well,' he drawled. 'Taking up where you left off with the old flames, are you, Alexandra?'

'Don't be ridiculous,' she snapped and whirled around towards the phone on the bedside table.

Max caught hold of her arm in a vice-like grip, stopping her in mid-stride. 'Tell Mr Steel that Mrs Channing is otherwise occupied with her husband.' He lifted his voice to speak to Rosie, who was waiting patiently outside the door.

'You had no right to do that,' Alexi spat as the house-keeper left to do his bidding.

'On the contrary, I have every right,' he told her in a low tone that somehow managed to strike a chill wave of fear through her. 'You belong to me, Alexandra Channing, and I won't allow you to run around with other men.'

'I don't belong to you,' she told him in no uncertain terms. 'I don't belong to anyone.' She swung away from him to start taking her case out of the wardrobe again. She would pack and leave; that would teach him just how much he owned her, she thought with fury.

Before she could put her hand on the case Max picked her up bodily to throw her on to the bed. For a moment she was too startled to move. She lay on her back, her dark hair tumbled around her pale face, her eyes wide with fear as she stared up at him.

'Did you sleep with Martin Steel last night?' he demanded in a tight, angry tone.

Alexi glared at him. How dared he ask her that question, as if she were the one who had something to be guilty about? The nerve of the man, after the way he had behaved. 'None of your damn business,' she breathed angrily as she started to sit up. 'I'm leaving you, Max, and I never want to see you again——'

He pushed her back down with a rough hand. 'You're not going anywhere,' he told her grimly. 'Not until I'm ready to let you go.'

'What are you going to do? Lock me up?' she asked contemptuously. 'You can't keep me here against my will.'

'I can do anything I want to,' he told her calmly. He turned away from her and closed the wardrobe doors with a decisive click. 'You see, I now own the premises of your precious Alexi-Miles studio.'

That statement met with a completely stunned silence.

He turned to face her and smiled coolly. 'And I do believe you are just about due to renew your lease?'

She swallowed hard. 'So what are you saying, Max?'

He looked at her pityingly. 'You're surely not that naïve? You know what it means; it means that you'd better be nice to me if you want favourable business terms.' He was speaking so matter-of-factly that for a moment Alexi wondered if she was hearing him correctly.

'You wouldn't stoop so low!' she whispered in a voice that trembled with angry disbelief.

'Try me.' He picked up her clothes from the floor and flung them at her. 'Fold your things and put them away where they belong,' he ordered flatly.

She made no movement, just continued to stare at him numbly.

'Do it now, Alexandra.' There was no arguing with that tone of voice.

She started to pick up the articles of clothing that had landed around her, her hands trembling, her mind still reeling as she took in the implications of what he had just said.

'Good girl.' He moved towards the door. 'From now on I expect you to behave in a manner suitable to being Mrs Channing,' he told her grimly. 'You can make a start right now. Clear up this mess and get yourself up to the lounge; we have guests.'

The eyes she turned up towards him were mutinous and resentful. How dared he treat her like this?

'Let me down in any way, and I will not hesitate to ruin your business, Alexandra. Not to mention the story I will give Georgia Gold.' The door opened and closed behind him with quiet finality.

The moment he had left she let the clothes fall around her to bury her head in her hands. Confusion and fear raced around inside her, then anger started to take over. She wasn't going to allow Max Channing to get away with treating her like this.

So what if he owned their business premises? She could afford to pay much higher rent now that her house was sold... But Miles couldn't, a little voice whispered inside. It would ruin him.

Her hands clenched into tight fists at her side. Maxwell Channing was a ruthless, cold-hearted swine. Oh, she would go along with him for the time being, but somehow she was going to make him pay. She was going to make Maxwell Channing very, very sorry, she vowed silently.

CHAPTER EIGHT

'THERE you are, darling.' Max stood up the moment she entered the lounge and walked towards her. He placed an arm through hers as he reached her side and turned to face the couple sitting on the sofa. 'I'd like to introduce you to two of my dearest friends.'

Alexi forced herself to smile while in reality all she wanted was to shake off Max's hand and place as much distance between them as she could.

'Paul and Carole Burns, this is my wife, Alexandra.'

Surprise flared inside Alexi. Carole Burns! The woman whom Joanne had told her about, the woman whom Max was supposed to be in love with.

'Pleased to meet you, Alexandra.' The woman smiled up at her. She was very attractive, and probably about thirty-one or -two. Her short blonde hair was immaculately styled, and she was wearing a red Chanel suit that fitted her slender figure to perfection.

Her husband stood up and reached out a hand to take Alexi's. He was a lot older than his wife—probably about forty-five—but still a very handsome man. 'We've heard a lot about you over the last couple of weeks, Alexandra,' he told her with a smile. 'Damn shame you couldn't have accompanied Max to New York.'

Alexi shot a look of disdain towards Max. He had visited Carole in New York, yet he hadn't even had time to phone her, she thought grimly.

'You live in New York?' she murmured, more to cover her silence than anything else.

Carole nodded. 'Paul and Max are partners in Holland Enterprises so they see a lot of each other... but I'm sure you already know all this.'

'No, I didn't actually,' Alexi said in a tight tone, while inside red-hot anger was sweeping through her as if a furnace door had just been opened. 'So Max wasn't the only one to make a profit out of the sale of my house,' she murmured bitterly.

'Sorry?' Carole looked at her blankly. 'I don't quite follow.'

'It's all right, Carole,' Max's voice interrupted smoothly. 'I'm afraid my wife doesn't understand a lot about business.'

Alexi swallowed hard, her hands clenching at her side with fury. 'Oh, I wouldn't say that.' Her voice was brittle. 'I happen to run a very successful business.'

'But for how long, my darling?' Max's voice, although smooth, held a distinct threat. 'I'd say the days of Alexi-Miles are numbered.'

Alexi's eyes blazed up at him.

'What would you like to drink, darling?' There was a glimmer of amusement on Max's face for a moment. Then he turned and walked towards the bar. 'Perhaps you should have a brandy; you're looking a little peaky.'

Alexi wanted to tell him to go to hell, but she forced herself to remain calm. 'Mineral water will do,' she told him briskly. She sat down in the armchair across from the other couple. 'I'm just a little tired. I've had a lot of late nights recently.' She smiled at them politely, but the comment was aimed at Max. She didn't want him to think she had been sitting in pining for him while he was away.

'It must have been lonely for you without Max.' Carole smiled sympathetically at her.

'Oh, no.' Alexi shook her head. 'I didn't have time to be lonely. I was out nearly every night having dinner with friends, or going to the theatre... There was always something going on.' It was a blatant lie. She had been in on her own every night since Max had been gone. It was her pride that wanted him to know that she didn't need him.

'Have you now?' Max handed her the glass of sparkling water, his eyes almost as cold as its frosty exterior. 'A guy could get jealous,' he murmured in a humorous tone as he turned towards the other couple. 'And there I was working my fingers to the bone and worrying about her.'

The words were spoken in such a mocking way that Alexi longed for a moment to lash out.

'Max was telling us all about your whirlwind wedding,' Carole said now. 'It certainly sounded romantic.'

'Do you think so?' Alexi wondered if this woman was in love with Max or if the attraction was all one-sided. Somehow she couldn't imagine that it was. Max was too powerfully attractive; no woman could help but be attracted to him. 'I think it might have been more a case of temporary insanity.' She lightened the comment with a laugh.

Carole laughed too. 'I think every woman has a few moments when she wonders if that was what really drove her to the altar.' She glanced at her husband beside her. 'Then they do something wonderful and you remember all over again why you married them.' For a moment there was a look of tenderness in the other woman's eyes that surprised Alexi. She didn't look like a woman who was in love with anyone other than her husband. 'It's our anniversary today, Alexandra. We've been married ten years,' the woman continued.

'Congratulations,' Alexi said with a smile, but she couldn't help wondering if Carole had married her husband before or after she had met Max.

'Which is why we are all going out tonight to the best restaurant in town.' Max joined the conversation and came over to lean against the side of Alexi's chair.

'Yes, I'm looking forward to that.' Paul glanced at his wristwatch. 'But now I think we should be getting back to the hotel, Carole. I have some business to attend to this afternoon.'

Carole rolled her eyes in mock-horror. 'Always business. I suppose you will be accompanying Paul?' She turned enquiring eyes up to Max, and as he nodded she sighed, then smiled at Alexi. 'I had planned to do a little shopping down Rodeo Drive this afternoon. Would you like to join me, Alexandra?'

Alexi could guess what business the men were going to be attending to. They would probably be at her house, measuring it up and rubbing their hands with satisfaction at another deal swung in their favour. The very idea made her blood boil. 'I'm sorry, Carole, but I have an important meeting myself this afternoon,' Alexi declined the invitation, knowing full well she wasn't in any kind of emotional state to go shopping with the woman.

'Ah, well, another time.' Carole stood up with her husband and Alexi politely got to her feet as well.

'I'll come down with you.' Max walked to the door with the couple.

'Goodbye, Alexandra, see you later,' Paul said in a friendly tone, and Carole smiled warmly at her as they went out.

Alexi sank back down in her chair feeling drained. Her mind kept returning to Carole's words—'Paul and Max are partners in Holland Enterprises'—and rage churned once more inside her. How dared Max...how dared he?

'Not a very impressive act, Mrs Channing.' Max's voice made her jump as he returned into the room. 'You'll have to do a better job than that if you want to convince people that we're a loving couple,' he drawled sardonically.

She glared at him. 'That's because we are not a loving couple,' she grated harshly. 'And I don't particularly care who knows it.'

'Really?' One eyebrow lifted. 'So I take it if Georgia Gold prints a very juicy story about us next week you don't care?'

The very idea made a cold spiral of alarm creep down her spine, but she forced herself to murmur, 'No, not really. Nobody believes that column anyway.'

'You don't think so?' Max sounded amused. 'She got all her facts straight about our wedding, didn't she?'

Alexi looked up at him, a horrible seed of suspicion growing. 'You gave her that story, didn't you?'

'Of course I did. Took a few minutes on the phone.' He smiled down at her. 'I thought it was a good idea to keep our roving reporter up to date. Never know when you might need her.'

Alexi swallowed hard. 'Meaning, I suppose, that you won't hesitate to update her.'

'Should it be necessary.'

'I hate you, Max,' she muttered furiously.

He shrugged powerful shoulders. 'Where are you going this afternoon?' His tone was crisp as he changed the subject.

'None of your damn business.' She got up from her chair and started to march towards the door. But he reached out and caught her arm in a vice-like grip.

'That's where you're wrong, Alexandra,' he purred in a deceptively soft tone. 'It's very much my business, especially if you have any plans to meet up with Martin Steel again.'

'I'll do what I damn well please,' she told him through clenched teeth.

'No, you won't,' he murmured and his blue eyes blazed furiously. 'You'll do as you are damn well told.'

'I don't know who the hell you think you are.' She tried to extricate herself from him, but it was useless struggling against all that power. 'You don't own me, Max.'

'Oh, yes, I do.' He pulled her sharply in against him, and the next moment he was lifting her off her feet. 'I thought I pointed that fact out to you just a little while ago.'

'What do you think you're doing?' she gasped, her heart racing with fear as he carried her out of the room and down the corridor towards their bedroom.

'I'm giving you a little refresher lesson on how you belong to me, Mrs Channing,' he grated drily as he dumped her down on their bed.

She stared up at him, her eyes wide and over-bright in her pale face as she watched him slowly remove his tie and then start to unbutton his shirt.

'Don't, Max.' Her voice trembled. 'I don't want you to come anywhere near me.'

He made no reply, just sat down next to her and removed his shoes.

'Don't, Max!' She started to turn and scramble over the other side of the bed, but he reached out an arm and caught her by the waistband of her jeans, pulling her effortlessly back beside him.

'Don't, Max.' He repeated her words in a mocking tone, then his lips came down against hers in a hard, crushing kiss.

She fought against him, her hands pushing with fury against the broad chest, her head twisting to get away from his lips.

He laced his fingers through her hair, forcing her head to stay still while he continued to kiss her. His lips left her mouth and trailed provocatively over the smooth pale skin of her cheekbones, then down the vulnerable curve of her neckline.

'Don't, Max; please don't.' Tears welled in her eyes as his hand left her hair and started to pull open the fasteners of her blouse.

He ignored her completely, his hand unfastening the front opener of her bra to expose the creamy softness of her breasts. Then his lips moved downwards.

'I missed you, sweetheart,' he murmured huskily as a few minutes later his lips returned to hers in a gentle caress.

The unexpectedly tender words and the warmth of his kiss stilled Alexi's fight, and instead of pushing him away her arms curved up and around his shoulders, her hands caressing the naked skin of his back.

She moaned softly as his hands moved to her breast, softly caressing her. Green eyes opened and for a moment locked with flame-blue. A smile softened his features as his eyes roved over her. Her dark hair was in wild disorder around the delicately pale face, the bright emerald-green eyes held a look of smouldering passion and total submission.

When the storm of passion had finally abated they both drifted into a deeply relaxed sleep. Max still held her in his arms; she felt safe, protected, cherished. For a while her mind was blank, the wrongs forgotten as she snuggled even closer to the warmth of his body.

He moved away from her to turn his wrist and glance at his watch. 'Have to go, honey.' He pulled away from her completely and got out of bed.

'Where are you going?' Immediately he left her she started to feel cold inside; the memories that had been blanked out for a short while started to flood back.

'A little business with Paul.' He fastened his trousers then reached for his shirt.

'Going to gloat over the purchase of my property?' she enquired coolly.

'No.' His voice was flat as he buttoned his shirt. Obviously this was a topic of conversation he was not interested in pursuing.

'Max?' She sat up, pulling the silk sheet firmly around herself and smoothing back her dark hair with a nervous hand as he flicked a look at her. 'Did you purposely go after me with the intention of getting my house?' She had to know his true intentions...had to hear him say it.

His lips twisted in amusement. 'Among other things, yes.'

She licked dry lips; it was strange how much it hurt. 'Revenge being one of those things, I presume?' Why was she torturing herself like this? she wondered. When she already knew the answers.

He moved to sit next to her on the bed. 'I started off just wanting your land and ended up wanting total possession of everything. You, the house——'

The shrill ring of the phone next to them cut the conversation dead, much to Alexi's relief. She didn't think she could bear to hear any more; already she felt on the edge of tears.

'That will be Paul, wanting to know where I am,' Max said grimly. 'Take it, Alexandra, will you? Tell him I'm on my way.' Max stood up to finish dressing as he spoke. 'We'll continue our talk later.'

Alexi didn't think she wanted to continue the discussion at all. She reached numbly for the phone.

'Hi, you're a hard person to get hold of these days.' The bright, cheery voice in her ear was unmistakable.

'Martin.' As she breathed his name in surprise Max turned to look at her.

'One and the same. Have you missed me?' Martin Steel was nothing if not confident. She knew he fully expected her to say yes.

'See you later.' Max turned at the door to look at her. His eyes glittered coolly. 'Don't forget we have a dinner appointment tonight. We leave at seven.' Then he was gone.

Alexi turned back to her conversation, her heart cold.

'Alexi, are you still there?' He was starting to sound impatient.

'Where did you get this number, Martin?' Even as she asked the question she knew the answer.

'Henri gave it to me.'

'Then you know that I'm married?' she asked flatly.

'Yes, I know. But Henri told me that you've made a mistake, married on the rebound.'

Alexi nearly laughed out loud. Martin was so arrogant; some things never changed. 'Sorry, Martin, but I married my husband because I love him.'

'So you're not going to leave him?'

'No, I have no intention of leaving him. I love him.' Even as she said the words she knew they were the truth. She did still love Max. As soon as he had taken her into his arms she had known it. In a way he was right; she did belong to him and she would stay as long as he wanted her to.

'So I suppose there is nothing else to say?' Martin said in a flat voice.

'Not if you want to talk about us getting back together,' she answered directly. 'But we can still be friends, Martin; we can still talk about your work.'

He laughed at that with genuine amusement. 'You know, Alexi, I do believe that's all we've ever talked about anyway.'

She smiled and relaxed. He was right, of course; there had never been anything deeper than that between them.

'So how's it going?' she asked and settled herself back against the pillows to listen.

Later, showered and changed into a light summer dress, she drove out along the coast road feeling much happier. Strange how making up her mind to stay with Max, no matter what, had made her feel so much better. Deliberately she put out of her mind all the reasons why she shouldn't stay and headed her car towards her father's house.

Somewhere mid-journey she got cold feet. She wasn't ready to face Henri's anger. He would only point out even more forcefully all the reasons why she should come home. Instead she found herself drawing up outside Miles's house. She owed it to him to tell him about the new developments with their business lease. Thinking again about what Max had done made a tremor run through her.

Nancy opened the door and her face lit up with a smile as she saw her friend. 'Alexi, how lovely; come in.'

Miles was sitting out by the pool reading. He jumped up immediately when he saw her. 'This is a pleasant surprise.' He pulled out a chair for her to sit down, and Nancy went to get them some drinks.

'I'm glad you came out today, Alexi——' Miles beamed at her '—because Nancy and I have something to tell you.'

'Oh?' She was hardly listening; her mind was elsewhere. 'Miles, I've come to tell you that Max has bought the deeds on our premises.' She blurted out the words.

She had half expected Miles to be angry, or even to look worried, but his reaction was completely unexpected. A look of deep relief flitted across his handsome features. 'Really?' He grinned at her. 'Oh, Alexi, I can't tell you how happy that makes me. I was getting worried about renewing that lease. I had the awful feeling that it was going to cost us a lot more this year and as business hasn't been so good...' He broke off as Nancy joined them with a tray of drinks.

'Great news, honey. Alexi's husband has managed to buy the deeds to our business premises.'

'That's wonderful.' Nancy looked questioningly at her husband. 'Have you told Alexi our good news yet?'

Miles shook his head and grinned. 'Nancy is pregnant, Alexi; that's why she's been feeling so sick recently.'

'Pregnant?' Alexi looked at her friends in surprise. Then her face broke into a bright smile. 'Congratulations, that's wonderful!'

It wasn't until she drove home that she started to worry again. Nancy and Miles had taken it for granted that Max would treat them right business-wise and that their problems were over. She hadn't had the heart to worry them with the truth.

What if Max charged them a ridiculous amount of money for next year's rent? Their budget would never stand it, and, even if they were able to find new premises, the price of moving could just finish them. Alexi felt sick with worry as she arrived back at Max's house, and this time she wasn't worried about herself. She was worried about Miles and Nancy and the new baby. Her actions from now on could ruin all of their lives.

'Cutting it fine, aren't you?' Max enquired as she entered the bedroom. He had just come out of the shower and had a bath-towel wrapped around his middle.

'I'll be ready on time.' Her voice was dull, her eyes filled with an anxious light.

'What's the matter?' He caught hold of her arm as she made for the bathroom.

'You know what's the matter.' She stared up at him. One eyebrow lifted, but he said nothing.

'Are you going to double the rent on our business?' The question burst out of her anxiously.

'Who knows?' He let her go and turned away from her.

She watched as he went through his wardrobe and took out a dark suit. His broad back was powerfully muscled; the towel sat low on lean hips. Even dressed in a towel Max had the power to turn her on.

'Did you meet with Martin this afternoon?'

The question took her by surprise. 'No.'

He turned a mocking eye over towards her. 'But then again you would say that, wouldn't you?' he drawled.

She went into the bathroom and closed the door.

A shower did nothing to alleviate the tense, angry mood she had lapsed into. The positive thoughts of earlier in the day had deserted her. How could she still love a man who didn't love her, a man who put business before people's feelings? Her stomach churned with a million mixed-up emotions.

Much to her relief the bedroom was deserted when she returned to it a little while later. She opened her wardrobe and ran an eye over the rows of clothing. She had no idea what to wear, but she wanted to choose something that would capture Max's attention. She selected a little red dress that was strapless and hugged her curvy figure lovingly.

She dried her long hair and left it loose around her face, then she applied a cherry-red lipstick to her lips and a little mascara to her large eyes. Finally, before she stepped into the dress, she put on the ruby and diamond necklace that Max had given her the day they had become engaged. The effect of the red dress and the gleam of deep red rubies and diamonds against her creamy skin was dynamite. Feeling more confident in herself, she picked up her beaded evening purse and went in search of Maxwell.

He was in the lounge, standing looking out of the large windows at the velvet black sea. He turned as he heard her enter, and for a moment his eyes moved over the feminine curves of her slender body, an appreciative male gleam in the blue eyes. 'You look lovely,' he murmured in a husky undertone, his eyes lingering on the necklace that she wore. Then before she had a chance to say anything he was glancing at his watch. 'Time we were going.'

They took the red Mercedes and travelled virtually in silence along the beauty of the coast road. Alexi, slanting a sideways glance at him, couldn't help but remember the night she had first met him, and how he had insisted on taking her home. It seemed like another lifetime, and yet it was only a few weeks ago. So much had changed in her life since then, yet the strange thing was she didn't regret any of it. She frowned at the thought. Sometimes she just didn't understand herself at all. Max had used her shamelessly and yet she still loved him.

He flicked a cassette into the stereo and the sound of Pachelbel's Canon filtered through the car. The same music as he had played that first evening. It had been a night very much like this one. The moon had been full. She also remembered the interest that he had taken in her house as they had driven up to it, the barbed comments.

She twisted around to look at him. 'What are you going to do with my house, Max?' she asked suddenly.

'You know what I'm going to do with it. I'm going to more or less knock it down to make way for a new leisure complex,' he answered steadily. 'More to the point, what are you going to do with *my* house?' he asked drolly.

She frowned, her heart still thudding painfully in her breast at the thought of her beautiful house being knocked down. 'What do you mean?'

'I mean, when are you going to redesign it for me? I did place the contract with you several weeks ago if I remember rightly.'

'I have some workmen lined up to come out to it next week,' she murmured.

'Good.' Max pulled up outside one of the most prestigious hotels in the area. 'Paul and Carole should be waiting for us... I said we'd pick them up—ah.' He smiled with satisfaction as the couple came out through the glass doors and walked in their direction.

Alexi watched them walk towards them. Carole looked extremely beautiful in a pale blue silk dress that seemed to float around her, showing a glimpse of long shapely legs as she moved.

Max was also watching Carole, she noticed out of the side of her eye.

The rear doors were opened and the other couple climbed in to join them.

They went to the same restaurant where they had celebrated their wedding with Miles and Nancy just over a fortnight ago. Tonight it was packed with the most elite of Hollywood's society, but even so they were immediately shown to the best table in the house.

'How did your shopping trip go, Carole?' Alexi asked as the men discussed a business deal in New York.

'It was wonderful.' Carole smiled at her in a conspiratorial manner. 'Paul would probably have a fit if he knew all that I bought. I got most of the shops to post the things on to me so that I wouldn't be laden down with them going home.' Her eyes alighted on the necklace that Alexi wore. 'I love your jewellery, Alexandra. Did you buy that here?'

Alexi fingered the necklace gently. 'It was a present from Max.'

'He has very good taste, hasn't he?' Carole remarked.

Alexi nodded. 'Have you known Max long?' She finally managed to ask the question that had been burning inside her all afternoon.

'He was originally Paul's friend from way back. I first met Max at our wedding.'

'I see,' Alexi murmured. Deep down she found herself wondering if the woman had instantly been attracted to him. In her imagination she could almost picture the scene: Carole looking extremely beautiful in white, Max looking devastating in a grey suit, the instant attraction that would have sprung up between them, the agony of the fact that Carole was about to be married to Max's best friend.

'Alexandra?' Max's voice penetrated her deep thoughts and she realised that everyone was waiting for her to place her order with the waiter.

'Sorry.' Hurriedly she glanced down at the menu and chose the first thing that caught her eye.

Max leaned across and filled her glass. 'You were miles away, honey,' he murmured in an undertone. 'Do you feel all right?'

For a moment she could almost imagine that he was concerned about her, but that of course was nonsense. The only thing that Max would be worried about was maintaining the appearance of a happily married couple. Who was he maintaining that appearance for? she wondered suddenly. Paul Burns? The idea made sense. Max would hardly want his best friend and business partner to guess how he felt about his wife.

'Alexandra?' Max's deep voice prompted a reply.

'I'm fine, Max.' Her voice sounded as troubled as she felt inside, and desperately she strove to keep up her cool appearance by continuing a light conversation with Carole.

Their meal arrived, but Alexi barely touched it. She did, however, drink her wine. It was her favourite, the wine that Max produced on his vineyard.

'Have you visited Max's vineyard in the Napa Valley, Carole?' she asked idly as she swirled the golden liquid around the crystal goblet. She probably shouldn't have asked that question, she thought dully, but she was getting past caring.

'Yes, Paul and I spent a weekend there last year. It was beautiful.'

'You brought Paul with you?' The question just slipped out. Somehow in her imagination she had pictured Max and her having an illicit weekend together there. Why else would Joanne be so positive about Max's involvement with the woman? Perhaps the girl had caught them stealing a kiss behind Paul's back?

'Yes, Paul came with me.' The woman sounded a little puzzled at the question.

Music started up behind them and some couples took to the floor.

'Would you like to dance, Alexandra?' Max's firm tone didn't sound as if he was going to accept a refusal.

She shrugged and got to her feet.

He led her into the middle of the floor, his hand gripping her arm painfully.

'You're hurting me, Max.' She frowned up at him as he turned her to face him and put an equally strong hand at her waist.

'Believe me, it's nothing compared to what I feel like doing,' he grated harshly. 'What the hell is the matter with you?'

She glanced up at him and her bright green eyes reminded him eloquently what was the matter with her. 'I'm sorry, Max; I'm just not good at pretending something that isn't true. I'm just not happy and I'm afraid it . .' Alexi trailed off and to her horror her eyes filled with tears. The intense hurt and the mixture of emotions tearing her apart showed clearly on her young face for a second before she gathered herself together again.

He put a finger over her lips in a strangely gentle movement. For a moment a host of different ex-

pressions crossed the handsome features. It was hard to
tell what exactly was going through his mind, but for a
moment Alexi thought she saw regret in those flame-
blue eyes. Then he gathered her into his arms and they
danced slowly, their bodies pressing close together.

When the music finished Alexi's heart was pounding
against her chest. She wanted to go back into his arms
for another dance, but he was already leading the way
back to the table.

The rest of the evening passed in a hazy blur. Carole
and Paul were pleasant company and, had circumstances been different, Alexi felt sure she would have
enjoyed the evening with them. As things were, though,
it was a relief when Max declared that it was getting late
and time that they should leave.

They dropped the couple off outside their hotel, de-
clining their invitation to join them in their room for a
drink. 'I'll see you early tomorrow, Paul, before you fly
back to New York,' Max said firmly. Then goodbyes
were exchanged and once more Alexi found herself alone
with Max.

She leaned her head back against the softness of the
seat and closed her eyes. Carole was leaving for New
York tomorrow, she thought, and she couldn't help but
feel more relaxed at that knowledge. She felt tired, the
fact that she hadn't slept very much at all the night before
catching up with her.

Max said nothing, just drove steadily through the
night, the powerful car gobbling up the miles easily.
When he pulled to a standstill outside his house her eyes
jerked open and she realised that she must have drifted
into sleep.

'You OK?' His voice sounded strained. He was obviously tired as well, she thought, remembering that he
had flown in from New York that morning.

'Yes, just tired.' She tried to smile at him, but it was a very weak kind of smile.

He opened his door and came around to help her out. She was grateful for that strong helping hand. Suddenly she just felt exhausted; whether it was emotional exhaustion or just lack of sleep she wasn't sure.

The night air was warm, scented with blossom and the tang of salt. She could hear the ocean as it gently swished in against the shore. It was so peaceful out here, she thought dreamily.

They walked slowly up the steps and into the house. It was cool inside; Rosie must have turned the air-conditioning up.

'Would you like a night-cap?' Max asked as he made his way towards the bar and poured himself a bourbon.

'I don't...' She caught the look in his blue eyes as he glanced over at her, and something about the way he looked at her made her change her refusal into an acceptance. 'I don't mind...a Perrier will do, please.'

He nodded. Alexi made her way towards the settee and sat down. She had the awful feeling that Max was going to say something she didn't want to hear. The feeling made her hand tremble alarmingly as she took her glass from him.

He frowned down at her. 'Do I frighten you, Alexi?'

It was the first time he had ever shortened her name and somehow, silly though it seemed, it made her even more nervous. She shook her head. He terrified her, but he didn't frighten her, she thought, and for a moment her lips twisted at the ridiculous admission. She loved him so much that it terrified her.

He took a deep drink of his bourbon and leaned back against the mantelpiece behind him. 'I'm sorry, Alexandra; I've made rather a mess of things.'

The admission made her head jerk up, her eyes wide and startled.

'I suppose at the back of my mind I had hoped...'
He broke off as his eyes took in the deathly pallor of
her skin. 'Anyway things haven't exactly worked out for
us, have they?'

She didn't know what to say to that. She twirled the
glass nervously between slender fingers. 'Did you think
they would?'

He grimaced. 'I guess I asked for that. You always
were direct; it was one of the things I liked about you
from the beginning.' He took another sip of his drink.
'Believe it or not, Alexandra, I never meant to hurt you.
At first it was just a game. You were a Rossini; I wanted
to win you over, get the house...' He trailed off and the
blue eyes became serious. 'Somewhere along the line the
game got out of hand, became deadly serious. I wanted
total possession or nothing.'

Alexi shivered at the tone in his voice. She hated
hearing him admitting so openly to all the awful things
her father had told her; somehow she had wanted to
bury her head from the truth, pretend that deep down
he really loved her. His brutal words stripped all the
shadows away, leaving nowhere for her to hide from
reality.

'I think, on reflection, that you were right to start
packing up your things today.'

Alexi could feel the room starting to swing around her
and she bit down so heavily on her lower lip that she
could taste blood.

'I had no right to use you the way I have done and
all I can say is I'm sorry.' His tone was hard and bleak
as if he was having the distasteful task of firing a long-
time employee.

She swallowed hard. 'What...?' She had to clear her
throat before continuing. 'What has brought about
this...this turn of thought? This afternoon you were
adamant that——'

'This afternoon I wasn't thinking rationally. Maybe I haven't been thinking rationally for the last few weeks, who knows?' He shrugged broad shoulders and his lips twisted in a bitter, cynical smile. 'It didn't quite dawn on me how unhappy I was making you until I saw the look of desolation on your face tonight.'

Alexi had a sudden urge to deny her unhappiness, to lie and tell him she was really all right, that she loved him and was happy to stay with him even though he didn't love her. But pride forbade her to say those things and she just continued to stare at him, wide-eyed, her heart thumping against her breast as if it was ready to explode.

Max turned away from her and headed for the bar to pour himself another drink. 'Go to bed, Alexandra,' he told her over his shoulder. 'I'll get Rosie to help you with your packing in the morning.'

Alexi literally flinched at that. 'There is no need. I can manage perfectly. Thank you.' Her voice sounded icily polite, as if she were talking to a stranger.

She put down her untouched glass of water. 'Goodnight, Max.' She walked with her head held high across the room.

'Goodbye, Alexandra.' She caught the softly spoken words as she closed the door behind her and she knew that there was no chance that Max would come and hold her in his arms tonight, or ever again.

CHAPTER NINE

'I WANT you to attend the Reads' party this evening.' Henri's voice was firm; it was an order, not a request.

'No.' Alexi's coffee-cup rattled back down on its saucer. The very thought made her feel sick inside.

'It's been two weeks, Alexi,' Henri snapped. 'You'll have to start socialising again, put your life back in order.'

'I don't feel like socialising.' She glared at her father across the breakfast table. It was two weeks since she had left Max and each day had felt like an eternity. Right at this moment she didn't feel as if her life would ever be happy again.

'Channing won't be at the party. I happen to know he's out of town,' Henri informed her calmly.

'I don't care. I still don't want to go,' Alexi maintained firmly, while inside her heart was beating double time at the mere mention of Max's name. How did her father know that he was away? She would have liked to ask where Max was...how long he had gone for, but she didn't dare show that much interest. Maybe he had gone back to England. The very idea made her blood run like ice through her veins.

Monica floated into the room in a white silk kimono and smiled at Henri. 'Good morning, darling,' she purred throatily and then bent to kiss his cheek.

Immediately Alexi stood up to leave. 'I'll have to be going or I'll be late for work.'

'You haven't eaten anything, Alexi,' her father growled. 'And I haven't finished speaking to you. Have you rung Herb Wilson yet?'

'I'm not hungry, Dad.' She started making for the door. 'And I haven't had time to ring Herb yet.'

As she closed the door behind her she could hear him saying, 'Well, get on to it today. Herb is a busy man and will be doing you a great favour by taking on your case.'

She closed her eyes and blinked away the sudden tears that had sprung into them. Herb Wilson was the lawyer Henri had found to handle her divorce for her and she certainly didn't feel that he would be doing her any kind of a favour. She just couldn't bring herself to start divorce proceedings. It was too soon; she needed more time to think about it.

As she walked across the cool, spacious hall the telephone rang on the table beside her. Alexi's eyes darted anxiously towards it and her heart lurched as hope flared that it just might be Max phoning for her.

The ringing stopped as Henri's secretary took the call. Alexi stood where she was, waiting to see if the secretary would come looking for her. Minutes passed and then there was the click as the receiver was replaced. Obviously the call had not been for her.

She picked up her briefcase and left the house feeling annoyed with herself. Every time the damn phone rang she hoped it was going to be Maxwell for her. When was she going to start getting some sense? When would she finally accept the fact that it was over?

She turned the radio on in the car as she drove to work, hoping that the conversation and music would help drown out the desperate feeling of loneliness that seemed to surround her. She missed Max so much that it was like a physical pain inside her. That pain had been there since he had told her to leave and it didn't show any signs of getting better.

She pulled into her parking space beside the Alexi-Miles studio and took a deep breath. Today was going to be better, she told herself firmly. She would deal with her work efficiently with no thoughts of Max and later this evening she would go hunting for a new apartment.

Moving out of her father's house would probably make her feel better. It wasn't that she didn't love her father—far from it. It was just that he was so insistent that she file for divorce straight away. Everything was remarkably black and white to Henri Rossini; he couldn't understand why Alexi couldn't just forget Maxwell Channing. He certainly would never understand the fact that she still loved him. Alexi could hardly blame him for that, though; she couldn't understand it herself.

Miles greeted her at their reception desk with a smile. She could see the sympathy in his expression and it irritated her. She wished that she hadn't told Miles anything about her breakup with Max. Not only was he now worried about the renewal of their lease, but he felt sorry for her. If there was one thing Alexi couldn't stand it was somebody feeling sorry for her.

'Morning, Alexi.' His eyes moved over her pale skin, the dark shadows under her eyes. 'How are you today?'

'Morning, Miles.' Her voice was crisp and she reached out a hand to take the morning mail from the reception desk. 'I'm fine.' She wished that he wouldn't treat her like an invalid; she wasn't sick, for heaven's sake.

She started to walk towards her office and he came after her quickly, catching hold of her arm and drawing her to one side. 'Alexi, I think maybe you should take some time off. This business with Max has really floored you and——'

'Floored me?' Alexi glared at him, her eyes wide and reproachful. 'Really, Miles, you can be quite melodramatic sometimes. There is nothing the matter with me. I'm quite capable of dealing with my work.'

'But are you capable of dealing with Max's work?'

'Max's work?' She stared at him quite blankly.

'Max has been on the phone; he wants to know when work is going to start on his house.'

'Oh!' That was all she could think of to say for a moment. Why hadn't he asked to speak to her when he had phoned? She felt so hurt for a moment that she could feel tears welling up inside her. 'Did he ask to speak to me?' She forced herself to ask the question.

Miles shook his head. 'But he did ask how you were,' he told her gently.

Alexi's mouth twisted in a crooked, bitter kind of smile. 'Very considerate of him.' She glanced up and caught their receptionist watching her with puzzled eyes. 'Let's go into my office, shall we? Before the whole damn world knows what a fool I've been,' she murmured and opened the door through to her domain.

'Don't be so hard on yourself,' Miles admonished sternly as he followed her in.

Alexi didn't answer him. She was busy flicking through her mail with eyes that were so blurred with tears for a moment that she could see nothing. She put the letters down on her desk and turned for the coffee-pot.

'I hope you won't be angry with me, Alexi, but I asked him outright about the lease.'

Alexi's hand stilled. 'What did he say?'

'He told me that he would speak to you about it soon.'

Red-hot anger swept through her. Max had no right to torment Miles with this worry. Her friend had enough to contend with now that Nancy was pregnant. 'It will be all right, Miles.' She looked around at him and her eyes sparkled with anger now, not sadness. 'I'm sure he won't do anything drastic.' She finished pouring the coffee, her hand none too steady. Maybe he wouldn't do anything awful, she told herself calmly. After all, he had threatened to go to Georgia Gold with the inside story of their marriage, and as yet there had been no reference to them in the woman's column. Alexi had

checked it every morning, her heart pounding with dread.
She was quite amazed that Georgia hadn't got hold of
the story yet.

'So do you want me to deal with Channing's house?'
Miles continued. 'I told him I'd send someone out there
this afternoon.'

'No, I drew up the plans; I'll see it through,' Alexi
told him firmly. 'I'll give Rosie a ring and arrange a time
to go out there with some workmen.'

'OK.' Miles glanced at his watch. 'I'll get back to work,
then. See you later.'

When the door closed behind him Alexi reached for
the phone and called Rosie. It wasn't so bad arranging
a time to go out there, because she knew that Max was
away. Had he been there she didn't think she could have
handled it at all.

Even so, when she drove out to Malibu she did feel
nervous and she did wonder if maybe she shouldn't have
been so foolhardy as to refuse Miles's offer to deal with
the job.

Rosie was delighted to see her. It was a far cry from
the morning when she had helped Alexi carry her suit-
cases out to her car. Then she had been silent, a look
of disapproval on her face. Today the kindly face was
all smiles. 'Come in, Mrs Channing; let me get you a
coffee.'

Before Alexi could refuse the woman was trundling
off to the kitchen, leaving her standing in the middle of
the lounge feeling most uncomfortable. Her gaze flicked
around the room. It was just the same as when she had
left it—luxuriously comfortable, fresh flowers in the
crystal vases. She found herself remembering the first
evening when she had come here for dinner, and a wealth
of sadness started up again inside her.

Rosie reappeared with her coffee. 'Sit down and make
yourself comfortable,' she instructed with a frown.

'I won't, thank you, Rosie. I'm waiting for the workmen to arrive so I can sort out exactly what's to be done today.' She took the coffee from the woman with a grateful smile.

'Oh, so you won't stay for some lunch?' The house-keeper looked disappointed. 'Mr Channing said you might be here for lunch.'

Alexi's eyebrows lifted at that. 'Mr Channing thought I would be here today?'

'Oh, yes. He said that he expected you might call this afternoon and he thought he might be back in time to see you.'

'Did he?' Max knew her so well that he knew she wouldn't pass her work here over to someone else. The thought of seeing him was alarming and yet at the same time exciting. 'Where is he, Rosie?' She allowed herself to ask the question that had been plaguing her all morning.

'He's had to go to San Francisco on business.' The doorbell rang and Rosie moved to answer it. It was the workmen, so the conversation came to an end as Alexi brought them around the house telling them exactly what she wanted them to do.

An hour later she was ready to leave, yet she found herself lingering, hoping that Max might come in.

She wandered down the corridor and stood in the doorway to the bedroom for a moment. The box that contained her engagement and wedding ring was just where she had left it on the dressing-table. Next to it was the long flat box that contained her ruby and diamond necklace, and then another box that she didn't recognise. She walked across to have a closer look.

The box had the Cartier name in gold letters. Alexi ran a hand curiously along it and then on impulse she opened the lid. It contained a magnificent gold bracelet with the inscription, 'All my love, Max'. Alexi closed the lid on it with trembling fingers. It hadn't taken Max long to find another woman... or maybe the bracelet was for Carole? Neither thought was very palatable and she turned away. All she could think about after that was leaving. She headed directly for the corridor; she was halfway across the room when Max appeared in the doorway.

She stopped dead, her heart racing, her mouth suddenly dry as her eyes locked on his handsome face.

'Hello, Alexandra.' The bright blue eyes moved over her features, the shadows under her eyes, the pale skin. He probably thought she looked dreadful, she thought resentfully.

'Hello, Max.' Her voice was remarkably cool.

His lips curved with a kind of cynical amusement. 'Fancy finding you in here.'

She didn't care for his sense of humour and that fact showed very clearly in the blaze of her bright green eyes. 'I'm here to redesign your décor, remember?'

'Oh, yes, I remember,' he murmured.

She crossed her arms in front of her in an unconsciously protective gesture. 'I'm glad I've bumped into you anyway.' She forced the words out, trying to sound as if she couldn't care less. 'I'm starting divorce proceedings. I thought you should know.'

'Very thoughtful of you.' His voice was dry and a pulse-beat flickered at the side of his strong jaw; otherwise there was no expression on his face.

He walked towards her and she took a step back, but she need not have worried because he wasn't interested in her; he was just placing his briefcase down on the bedside table. 'Now that you're here you may as well have this.' He opened the case and riffled through the contents to take out a brown envelope. 'Here.' He handed it across to her, his manner vaguely impatient.

She took it from him, a puzzled frown marring her smooth features. 'What is it?'

'Open it and see.'

For one awful moment she thought that the legal-looking documents inside were divorce papers. 'It's the deeds on your business premises,' Max told her brusquely.

She looked up at him in complete amazement and he shrugged. 'I've had them made over to you. They're of no use to me.'

She was completely overcome for a moment. 'Why have you done this?'

'I told you—I don't need them. Believe it or not, I never intended to use them against you. They were bought because I knew you were worried about the lease.' He sounded almost gruff now.

'Thank you, Max,' she whispered huskily, relieved beyond words that she no longer had to worry about the lease on their business. A warm feeling started to glow inside her. Max had bought them especially for her! Did that mean something...? Did he care a little bit about her?

'If there is one thing I don't deserve it's your thanks,' he answered her quietly.

She swallowed hard. 'Well, you have them anyway.'

He snapped his case shut. 'So have you started to see Martin again?'

The question surprised her. 'I've seen him, but——'

'It's all right, Alexandra. I shouldn't have asked you such a personal question,' he cut across her. Then he glanced at his watch. 'I really have to go, anyway. I have a meeting with Paul in an hour.'

She had been about to say that she wasn't seeing Martin in the way he meant, but his statement surprised her and she frowned. 'I thought that Paul and Carole had gone back to New York.'

He shook his head. 'Paul and I have had a slight difference of opinion and it's led to complications.'

'I see.' Alexi felt like asking if their difference of opinion was over Carole, and coldness crept back into her heart. Maybe the woman had decided to leave Paul and move in with Max...hence the inscription on the bracelet, and the speed with which Max had asked her to leave. She didn't dare to voice the question. There was silence for a moment while they both stared at each other.

'Are you going to the Reads' party this evening?'

The question didn't surprise Alexi. The Reads' party was a big social occasion. Anyone who was anyone would be attending. 'I don't know...maybe. Are you?'

He shook his head. 'Haven't the time.'

'Probably just as well we're not both going with different partners; our secret would be well and truly out then,' she murmured thoughtfully.

'Alexandra, sooner or later we're going to be spotted out with different people. Our marriage is over and it's only a matter of time before everyone knows it.'

Alexi flinched at the blunt statement and her skin paled even more visibly.

There was a tap at the door at that moment and one of the workmen put his head around the door. 'Sorry to disturb you, Miss Rossini, but I want to ask you about the colour co-ordination for the hallway.'

'OK, I'll be there in a moment,' Alexi told him, and he disappeared again.

'Didn't take you long to go back to your maiden name,' Max drawled, a dry note in his words.

She shrugged. 'I've hardly been Mrs Channing long enough for people to remember it. Anyway, as you've just said, our marriage is over.' Then she walked away, her head held high. He would never have guessed how much it hurt for her to say those words.

She was exhausted when she arrived home that evening; her encounter with Max had totally drained her. The last thing she needed was a lecture from Henri, but that was exactly what she started to get when she told him she still hadn't rung their lawyer.

'And what about this party tonight? Are you too afraid to go to that too?' he blazed as she walked away from him across the hallway and up the stairs.

'I'm not afraid, Henri; I just don't particularly want to go.' She remained calm, although inside she felt ready to scream.

'Well, that's just too bad,' her father said crisply, 'because I told Martin that you would see him there.'

'You had no right to do that.' Alexi turned around to glare at him furiously. 'I've told Martin that I'm not interested in continuing where we left off, and anyway, you always said you didn't like me seeing Martin. Why the sudden change of heart?'

'The sudden change of heart is because I'd prefer you to be with Martin Steel than Max Channing.' The doorway at the other side of the hall banged closed behind him.

The simple truth was that he would rather she saw anyone other than Max, Alexi thought as she continued up the stairs.

Once in the privacy of her bedroom she leaned back against the door and heaved a sigh of relief. Maybe she would go out this evening; anything would be better than staying in and irritating Henri further.

She opened her bag and took out the envelope with the deeds to her business in it. For a moment she stared at it thoughtfully. Why had Max had such a change of heart? Was it because he no longer had anything to gain by keeping her under his influence? After all, he owned her house now, and he had well and truly managed to upset Henri, and finally it looked as if he was going to get the one woman he loved.

She shook her head. She didn't know if Carole was going to leave Paul for him. That was just a surmise; there was no proof. What about that bracelet? a little voice whispered. Wasn't inscribing something with his name proof enough that his love for the woman was now out in the open?

Alexi walked over to the dressing-table and put the deeds firmly in a drawer. She wasn't going to think about it any more. She was going to get changed and go out and have a good time.

Some time later when she had showered and changed into a strapless black evening dress, she began to doubt very much that she would have a good time. She studied her reflection in the cheval-mirror with a critical eye. She had lost a little too much weight recently and was starting to look skinny. Her skin was far too pale, her eyes too large for the delicate oval face. She turned away from the mirror and picked up her wrap and evening purse.

There was no point worrying about her appearance anyway. There would be no one who really mattered at the party. Max would not be there. But that was where she was wrong. Max was there and he was not alone.

CHAPTER TEN

'YOU look fabulous.' Martin Steel looked her over in a way that made her feel most uncomfortable. It was as if he was deciding which part of her he wanted to eat first.

'Thanks.' Her voice was flat and her eyes, instead of being riveted to his tall, well-built frame, were roving around the room. 'There are a lot of people here; looks like the Reads have invited the whole of Hollywood,' she remarked idly.

'The same old crowd,' Martin agreed. 'I'm quite glad to be going back to England at the end of this week even if it is raining there.'

'You're going back to England next week?' She turned her eyes towards him, more interested now.

'Yes, well, we haven't finished the film yet, you know.' He grinned at her. 'Unexpectedly, Henri was good enough to allow me this short break. They're shooting around me at the moment, but if I'm not back soon it will hold up the production and cost a small fortune into the bargain.'

'Is Henri planning to return with you?'

'Sure is.' Martin smiled. He had boyish good looks—'cute' was how most women described him. Compared to Max, he was quite ordinary, Alexi found herself thinking. She frowned at the thought.

'Want to come back with me?'

'Pardon?' The question took her completely by surprise and she stared at him blankly.

169

'I asked if you would like to come back to England with me,' he said with a smile.

'Henri put you up to asking me that, didn't he?' she asked with a shake of her head.

'No.' Martin hesitated then shrugged. 'He's given me his blessing to start dating you again...and I suppose he did kind of mention it would be nice to have you along with us for a while.'

Alexi's lips tightened. 'He'd suggest anything to make sure I was away from Max.'

'And you don't want to be away from him,' Martin stated drily.

She looked down at the delicate champagne flute in her hand. 'I love him,' she answered simply.

'Yet you left him. Not much of a love.' Martin's voice was dry. She glanced up at him, her eyes filled with pain.

He grimaced. 'Sorry, sweetheart; I guess I'm just a little jealous. I wish I'd stirred up those kinds of emotions in you.'

Before she had time to answer that she noticed that Georgia Gold was heading towards them, a purposeful gleam in her bright eyes. 'Oh, no,' Alexi groaned.

'Hello, Alexi, where is your husband this evening?' The woman was nothing if not direct.

Before Alexi had time to say anything, Martin answered for her. 'Max has been held up on business. I'm standing in as escort.'

Alexi flicked a surprised look at her friend.

'Really...?' Georgia drawled the word with a certain amount of disbelief. 'I had heard that things were not quite as they should be in the Channing house—namely that you have moved home, Alexi.'

Alexi forced herself to smile as if the other woman's words amused her. 'Have you, now...? Is this the gist of your next story?'

'Well, I was rather hoping to have you confirm it as true before I went ahead.' Georgia watched her hopefully.

'That is surprising. You've never bothered to get your facts straight before, Georgia. What has come over you?' Alexi drawled, more than a hint of sarcasm in her voice.

The other woman's face clouded with anger briefly before she cloaked it again with a charming smile. 'Oh, I get my facts from very reliable sources. I got this bit of information from someone very close to you indeed.' Confident that her parting shot had caused a flutter of anxiety in Alexi, she strolled away with a rather smug expression on the beautiful features.

Who had told Georgia that she had moved back home? The question burned through Alexi's brain, closely followed by the answer...Max. It had to be Max; there was no one else. She knew Miles wouldn't have said anything and certainly her father wouldn't—he wanted just to pretend her marriage had never taken place. She felt so disappointed and upset that for a moment she couldn't answer Martin when he asked her to dance. She hadn't thought that Max would have been so callous as to announce the breakup of their marriage. She had thought when he had given her the deeds to her property that he had mellowed towards her a little. Perhaps a little part of her had hoped that he was missing her.

'Alexi, would you like to dance?' Martin repeated his question.

She nodded. At least if they were on the dance-floor she wouldn't have to struggle to concentrate on his conversation. It was ridiculous to feel so upset. Why was she so naïve as to keep hoping that Max cared a little about her? He had used her; he had admitted that quite openly. He didn't love her at all—that much was also very clear—yet deep down she just couldn't accept those facts.

When they got on the dance-floor the music changed from a fast rhythmic beat to a slow romantic one. Martin grinned down at her. 'My lucky night,' he murmured as he gathered her in to his arms.

She didn't protest as he held her close; her mind was on Max and their marriage. She even twined her arms up and around Martin's neck. She rested her head against his chest for a while, her heart heavy.

'This is just like old times,' Martin murmured against the softness of her dark hair.

His words brought her back to reality suddenly and she pulled away from him a little. 'But it's not old times, Martin. I'm married, remember?'

He nodded. 'You won't let me forget.'

She smiled up at him. 'But thanks for standing up to Georgia for me; I do appreciate it.'

'Any time.'

Martin's reply was lost on her because her attention had moved towards the crowds surrounding the dance-floor. She had the uncanny notion that someone was watching her; she could feel it so strongly that it was almost as if someone had reached out and tapped her shoulder. She moved her face a little to the left and her eyes met with a flame-blue gaze that blazed directly at her.

'Max.' She murmured his name under her breath and for a moment she was transported back in time to the Jameses' party. She remembered the way their eyes had met across the crowds and held, just as they were doing now. The same feelings rushed through her; elation, an attraction that was so powerful that it made her feel dizzy, breathless, afraid.

'Alexi, are you OK?' Martin's voice seemed to be coming to her from a distance. All her senses were tuned in on Max. He looked so incredible. No man had ever had such a power over her that she'd felt like just walking over to him and flinging herself into his arms.

'Alexi?'

She had to force herself to look away and back at her partner. 'Max is here,' she told him simply.

'Is he, now?' Martin looked a little annoyed. 'I suppose that means that I've lost my date for the rest of the evening.'

About to remind him that she had not been 'his date' to start with, she changed her mind and instead glanced back in Max's direction with uncertainty. Who was he with?

He was looking away from her now and talking to his companion. Alexi's heart sank totally; it was almost as if someone had drained her of all energy for life with one fell swoop. Max was with Carole.

'Come on, I'll get you a drink,' Martin murmured as he noticed how pale Alexi had gone suddenly.

Much to her relief he led her off the dance-floor in the opposite direction to Max. She couldn't have endured a polite conversation with him and Carole.

Her hand trembled slightly as she took the champagne glass from Martin's outstretched hand.

'You've sure got it bad,' he remarked drolly, and she shot him a look of irritation. 'Sorry, Alexi, but I'm afraid you're not being very sensible about all this. Some marriages are just a mistake from start to finish. Hell, you only have to look around this room to know that; most of the people in here are on their second and third marriages, maybe even more. This is Hollywood; you are not the first and you will not be the last to make a mistake where relationships are concerned.'

'And here endeth the first lesson,' Alexi murmured drily. She swirled the golden liquid around the crystal glass and inside she was remembering that first conversation with Max. He had joked about their getting married and then divorced within a ludicrously short space of time. Or rather she had thought it was a joke; little had she realised that he had been deadly serious. She swallowed hard and looked around the room, feeling suddenly claustrophobic.

'I wonder where Henri has got to?' Martin remarked idly. 'I should have thought he would be here by now.'

Alexi shuddered, the thought of Max and her father under the same roof giving rise to palpitations. 'I could do with some fresh air, Martin.' She leaned across and placed her drink on the table next to them. 'Excuse me for a moment.'

He let her go, his eyes watching her progress as she fought to get through the heaving crowds then finally made it to the open patio doors.

The large house backed out towards the ocean. The night air was soft and warm. There was a gentle whispering sound as the water swished in and out from the shore. Alexi moved to the end of the terrace beyond the golden spill of light from the house, and into the velvet black shadows of the night.

The sound of the ocean was strangely therapeutic to her frayed nerves. She leaned against the stone balustrade and stared down at the moonlit beach. It was deserted, eerily beautiful in the cool silver light that played over the ocean.

She found herself remembering the evening she had walked on the beach with Max, and her eyes filled with the glitter of tears for a moment.

The muted sound of music grew louder for an instant as the door behind her opened then closed. She turned, half expecting to see Martin, but it was Max who stood alone in the warm flood of light from the house. His eyes moved towards her shadowy form. 'Getting some fresh air, Alexandra?' His voice held a strained note that was most unusual for Max.

'No, I'm playing truant.' She took refuge in flippancy and turned away from him to stare back out towards the sea. She hoped he would go back inside now that he had accidentally found her out here.

'Who from?' He walked over to stand beside her, much to her discomfiture. 'Martin or your father?'

'Everyone.' She turned her eyes rather pointedly towards him.

He didn't take the hint and leave; instead he said smoothly, 'In that case I'll join you for a few moments. I could do with escaping the heat for a while myself.'

Alexi's mouth tightened with annoyance. 'I thought you weren't coming tonight?' she said stiffly.

'I changed my mind,' he said calmly. 'That's not just a woman's prerogative.'

Meaning that she also had changed her mind. She shrugged lightly. 'I just wish you had had the decency to warn me you would be here, then I could have avoided the function.'

'Alexandra, I intend to be in California for quite some time. I do not intend to check with you every time I attend a party or a dinner.' He sounded angry now. 'You will just have to get used to the fact that we are going to bump into each other.'

He was right, but somehow she refused to accept it. Anger was building up to an intolerable level inside her. In her mind Max was deliberately trying to humiliate her by turning up at this party with Carole. Then there was the information he had given Georgia. 'Did you tell Georgia Gold that I've moved home?' she asked in a voice that trembled slightly with fury.

'No.' His answer was unequivocal, yet she didn't believe him.

She stared stonily out at the ocean and the silence stretched. Only now the lapping of the waves against the shore was not a soothing sound; it seemed to fill the air with tension.

'I take it you don't believe me?'

'Damn right I don't.' She swung to face him, her eyes flashing fire in the cool of the moonlight. 'I think you've tried your level best to hurt me as much as you can. I think that just because my name is Rossini you have used me shamefully, that you hate me with a vengeance, and now you are intent on publicly humiliating me.'

His eyes moved over the porcelain paleness of her skin and down to where the black dress dipped at her breast, showing how it heaved a little at the short angry breaths she was taking. 'Maybe that was true at the beginning.' He shrugged broad shoulders, his manner calm. 'Certainly when I first met you I had no compunction about...using you. I wanted the land your house stood on, and your stubborn refusals to sell stood in the way of me and a multi-million-pound development. The fact that your name was Rossini justified what I did.' He paused for a moment, his eyes on the soft curve of her lips. 'Marriage was never in my plans at that stage. I was going to seduce you, get you between the sheets, and basically entice and beguile you into selling that house and land to me. Then once I got what I wanted I was going to walk away without a backward glance or regret. Unfortunately in reality those plans were not so easy to carry out.'

She swallowed hard on a knot of tears that threatened to explode. She wanted to place her hands over her ears like a child refusing to listen to something she didn't want to hear. 'I don't really want to know, Max——'

'Maybe not, but I want you to know.' He interrupted her forcefully. 'Maybe then I'll be able to sleep nights.'

Her eyes clouded in puzzlement. 'You lost sleep over all this?' Somehow she had imagined it wouldn't have cost him a thought.

'Contrary to what you might think, I am not completely without feelings. Yes, I've lost sleep,' he murmured huskily. 'You see, I had all these plans before I met you. I was going to get exactly what I wanted. I was going to get that land, and if I upset Henri Rossini into the bargain it was bingo. Then I met you and from the moment our eyes met at that party my plans started to dissolve.'

'You mean I wasn't so easy to get between the sheets as you'd thought,' she murmured bitterly.

He smiled. 'Yes, there was that, but I'm sure if I'd persevered for a while longer...' He let his voice trail off provocatively.

Her mouth twisted with distaste. 'But time was money, isn't that the saying, Max?'

He hesitated. 'No, that saying is not relevant to what I'm telling you.'

'And the moon is made of cream cheese,' she finished for him mockingly.

'I don't blame you for being bitter, Alexandra. I took advantage of you when you were at your most vulnerable and that——'

'What do you mean, my most vulnerable?' She cut across him, frowning.

'I mean that you had just broken up with the man you loved. Martin had gone off to England without you and you were vulnerable. Enter Maxwell Channing for the kill,' he finished drily.

For a moment she just stared at him. He thought that she had married him because she was on the rebound. He didn't realise how she felt about him! It seemed incredible that he should imagine for one moment that

Martin would hold any kind of attraction for her after she had married him.

The silence was broken by the door opening behind them and then a deeply rasping voice demanded to know what was going on.

Even before she turned to face him, Alexi was well aware that it was her father, and her heart thudded so hard that it took her breath away as she turned around.

Henri Rossini stood in the pool of light from the house. It gleamed over his hair and threw his face into sharp focus. The expression on that face was one that struck terror in Alexi's very soul.

'Well, I'm waiting for an explanation, young lady.' Alexi felt as if she were sixteen again. But for the fact that she was struck dumb with fear it would have been funny.

'Your daughter and I are having a private conversation.' Max's voice was quite calm, with no hint of panic and certainly no fear.

'Stay away from my daughter, Channing.' Henri Rossini's tone dripped with venom.

'Is that some kind of a threat?' Max merely sounded amused.

Henri Rossini took a couple of steps forwards and Alexi spoke up for the first time.

'Please, Father, please don't make a fuss. I'm coming inside now.' The words rushed into one another in a clumsy attempt to smooth over things.

'Good idea,' Max murmured. 'Go back inside, Alexandra. I would like a private word with your father.'

'No.' Alexi shook her head, her eyes wide with horror. There was no way she wanted to leave the two men alone; there was no telling what would happen.

'Go inside, Alexi.' Her father reinforced the order in a tightly controlled voice.

When she still made no movement Max gave her a little push. 'Go on,' he said gently. 'Everything will be all right.'

She left them very unwillingly. Her heart pounded as she stepped back through the door into the crowds again. Her hand shook as she picked up a glass from a table and tried to look nonchalantly around the room. But her gaze kept returning to the door. What if Henri tried to hit Max? The thought sprang unbidden to mind and her heart went into a frenzy of fear. Her father was a strong man, but nowhere near as strong as Max. If Max swung at him in turn he could kill him.

Dear God, please don't let either do anything stupid, she prayed silently. She loved them both so much that the fear was unbearable.

It seemed an eternity before the door opened again and Max came out. His face was serious, the grooves at the side of his mouth more pronounced than she had ever seen them. She swallowed hard and found she was so afraid that she couldn't move quickly enough to get to his side and ask what had happened. Indeed, before she could move Max had stridden across the room and left by the main entrance without a backward glance.

She bit down on the softness of her lower lip and forced herself to move towards the doors to the terrace. There was a little part of her that half expected to find her father lying on the ground as she went outside. Instead he was standing where she had left him, a curious expression on his face.

Relief flooded through her. 'Are you all right, Henri?'

He didn't answer immediately; he seemed completely lost in deep thought.

'Henri?' She put a gentle hand on his shoulder and he looked at her at last.

'You know I ... care about you, don't you, Alexi?'

The question startled her so much that it took a moment to answer.

'Yes, of course.' She frowned. 'What on earth is——?'

'You still love him, don't you?' His eyes were grave as he turned to face her.

She didn't even need to think about that. 'Yes. I love him with all my heart.'

'Then go after him.'

For a second Alexi thought she had misheard.

'Go after him, Alexi.' He gave her a push towards the door.

'Henri, you've been telling me for weeks to keep away from him... What on earth is going on?'

His lips curved in a humourless smile. 'We are all entitled to our mistakes.'

Alexi frowned, wondering suddenly if her father was sick. 'I'll get Monica,' she said at last.

Henri shook his head. 'Monica and I have split up... She was another little mistake of mine. I caught her feeding information to Georgia Gold on the telephone this evening.'

'Monica!' Suddenly it clicked into place. It was Monica who had told Georgia about her moving home, not Max.

A spark of happiness lit Alexi's eyes for just a moment, then died. So what? Max was innocent of one little thing, but he had still used her, and he still didn't love her.

'Are we going to stand out here all night?' Henri suddenly regained his composure and linked his arm through hers. 'I have a little business to discuss with a certain Paul Burns.'

'Paul Burns?' Alexi's mouth literally dropped open. 'That's Max's business partner.'

'And soon to be mine. Max has offered to sell out his share in the sports-complex deal at a very reasonable price.'

'Max is selling out his share in my house?' Alexi felt as if the whole world were starting to spin dizzily around her. It was just all too much to take in.

'My dear, you are starting to sound like a parrot.' Henri led the way indoors. 'Now perhaps you would be good enough to point out Paul before you go after that man of yours?'

Automatically Alexi's eyes searched the room to do as she was told. But inside her mind was racing around in utter confusion. She spotted Paul easily. He was on the dance-floor with his arms wrapped around Carole.

'I don't understand this.' Alexi stopped where she was, her heart thundering. 'I thought that Max was here with Carole... I thought he loved her.'

Henri looked down at his daughter, a hint of impatience in his eyes. 'My darling daughter, Max Channing is crazy about you. Why else would he give up such a lucrative deal to me?'

Alexi swallowed hard, hardly daring to believe what Henri had said.

Henri shook his head and then grinned. 'Go and get him.'

Alexi drove with speed along the coast road out to Malibu. Her hands were firm on the wheel and her driving was perfect. She dared not think about the words her father had spoken to her before she had left the party. She couldn't allow herself to really believe that Max cared about her. All she knew was that she had to see him.

Max's car was parked outside his house when she pulled up, and she heaved a sigh of relief at the sight of it. A little part of her had been frightened that he wouldn't be at home.

The night air was silent and the only sound seemed to be the beating of her own heart as she walked up the steps to the front door. She hesitated for a moment. She didn't really want to ring the bell and wake Rosie; the idea made her even more nervous. She would look such a fool if she demanded to see Max and then he turned her scornfully away. Her hands clenched into tight fists at the very thought. She turned her head and noticed that the lounge lights were still on. Max was obviously still up. On impulse she walked around the veranda, intending to knock quietly on the glass doors at the back.

To her surprise the glass doors were open. She stood looking into the lounge for a full minute before she realised that it was empty.

Her heart thumping nervously, she turned and looked down at the beach below her. For a while she could see nothing; everything was cast into velvet shadow as the moon sailed behind a cloud. Then the cool silver light reappeared and for a moment she could see him clearly, standing at the water's edge, his back towards her as he stared out to sea.

She didn't hesitate now, but slipped her shoes off to hurry down towards the sands.

He didn't hear her approach him and she stood for a few moments behind him, trying to regain her composure to be able to speak to him.

'Max.' For a second she didn't think he had heard her; her soft voice seemed to catch on the breeze and dissolve into the merest whisper. Then he turned slowly to face her.

'Alexi.' He shook his head as if she were an apparition that had appeared with the silver of the moon and would fade as it disappeared behind the clouds.

His eyes moved over her slender body in the black evening dress. The skirt fluttered around her long legs as the gentle breeze playfully caught it. Her long hair moved against the creamy bare skin of her shoulders, and she put up a hand to brush it impatiently away from her eyes.

'What are you doing here?' His voice sounded strained. His hands clenched into tight fists at his sides as he watched her.

She swallowed hard. 'I'm here because . . . I'm here because...' She shook her head, irritated beyond measure by how nervous and unsure of herself she sounded. She tilted her head up at a proud angle and forced herself to meet those blue eyes. 'I'm here because I love you, Max.' There, she had said it. Strangely enough she felt an immediate sense of relief at having spoken those words to him.

For a moment he said nothing, then just as she was starting to feel as if her confidence was deserting her he took a step forwards. 'Alexi.' He shook his head wordlessly and the next moment she was folded into his arms.

Her heart thundered in her breast as she clung to him, breathing in the familiar tangy scent of his cologne, burying her head against the softness of his shirt. They clung to each other so tightly that neither had the breath to say anything. Then Max lifted his head from her hair.

'You don't know how long I have ached to hear you say those words,' he murmured in a deep, husky voice. 'I love you so much. Have done, I think, from the moment our eyes first met.'

She bit down on the softness of her lip. 'Am I dreaming, Max, or did you just say that you loved me?' she whispered.

He twined his fingers through her hair and smiled gently. 'Love you with every bone in my body,' he reassured her. 'Love the way you walk, the way you talk, that proud way you tilt your head sometimes when you look at me——'

Alexi placed a finger over his lips and he kissed it tenderly. He was going too fast; she could hardly take it all in. 'I thought you hated me.' Her voice shook with the pain of those memories. 'I thought you only married me because of business and because you couldn't have the woman you really loved. I thought that you and Carole——'

'Carole is nothing but a business associate's wife.' Max cut across her impatiently. 'I thought I made that clear when we were in the Napa Valley. Joanne was beside herself with jealousy, Alexandra. She's had a teenage crush on me for years... I thought she had grown up until she so childishly told you a pack of lies.'

Alexi stared up at him, her breath caught in her throat as hope lit the bright green of her eyes.

'I married you because I loved you. No other reason. Oh, I know my intentions were not so honourable to begin with; I've already told you that and I deeply regret it. But as soon as I started dating you those plans started to take a back seat to my feelings for you. I wanted the house, but I wanted you even more.'

'Which is why you've offered Henri your share of the new complex deal on my land?' she asked with a wondering shake of her head.

He nodded. 'The deal means nothing compared to losing you. I've missed you so much, sweetheart.'

She flung herself into his arms and turned her lips for his kiss, happiness flooding through her in delightful waves. It was a while before they spoke again.

Max lifted his head and smiled into her eyes. 'I only came to the party tonight to beg you to come back to me,' he murmured. 'Then I saw you in Martin Steel's arms and I thought it was useless to plead.'

Alexi had to laugh at that. 'There is nothing between Martin and me. The idea is almost as inconceivable as you pleading.'

'You think I wouldn't beg?' One eyebrow lifted and he looked amused for a moment. Then he reached into the pocket of his dark jacket and took out a box. 'Please will you come back to me, Alexandra, and be my wife?' The words were spoken with deep sincerity now, the amusement gone as he waited for her to reply.

'Oh, Max.' She reached up to kiss him again. 'I love you so much,' she whispered against his lips.

'Then I can give you this?' He pulled away from her to open the box. Inside was a gold bracelet that sparkled and shimmered under the bright moonlight and Alexandra's tears.

'With all my love,' he whispered softly.

Later, as they walked hand in hand back up towards the house, Alexi asked him curiously, 'What did you say to my father tonight?'

When Max merely smiled she continued hurriedly, 'I mean, apart from appealing to his more mercenary side with a good business deal, what did you say to make him change his mind about you?'

'I told him that my father had forgiven him for what he did. That he had built a very good life for himself back in England and bore him no malice.' Max pulled her closer in against his side. 'I think that a lot of the hatred Henri felt for me was based on a deep guilt.'

'And has your father forgiven him?' she asked softly.

'Yes, he has.' Max turned her to face him. 'More to the point, have you forgiven me?'

'For what?' she asked with complete sincerity. 'I've forgotten already.'

'For taking total possession of everything you have, for——'

She placed her hand gently over his mouth and smiled up at him mischievously. 'I was rather hoping that you would do it again,' she whispered, then curled her hands up and through his hair. 'Maybe tonight?'

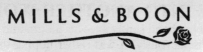

ESCAPE INTO ANOTHER WORLD...

...With Temptation Dreamscape Romances

Two worlds collide in 3 very special Temptation titles, guaranteed to sweep you to the very edge of reality.

The timeless mysteries of reincarnation, telepathy and earthbound spirits clash with the modern lives and passions of ordinary men and women.

Available November 1993   Price £5.55

MILLS & BOON

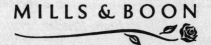

4 FREE

Romances and 2 FREE gifts just for you!

*You can enjoy all the
heartwarming emotion of true love for FREE!
Discover the heartbreak and happiness,
the emotion and the tenderness of the modern
relationships in Mills & Boon Romances.*

*We'll send you 4 Romances as a special offer
from Mills & Boon Reader Service,
along with the opportunity to have 6 captivating
new Romances delivered to your door each month.*

Claim your FREE books and gifts overleaf...

An irresistible offer from Mills & Boon

Become a regular reader of Romances with Mills & Boon Reader Service and we'll welcome you with 4 books, a CUDDLY TEDDY and a special MYSTERY GIFT all absolutely FREE.

And then look forward to receiving 6 brand new Romances each month, delivered to your door hot off the presses, postage and packing FREE! Plus our free Newsletter featuring author news, competitions, special offers and much more.

This invitation comes with no strings attached. You may cancel or suspend your subscription at any time, and still keep your free books and gifts.

It's so easy. Send no money now. Simply fill in the coupon below and post it to -
Reader Service, FREEPOST, PO Box 236, Croydon, Surrey CR9 9EL.

NO STAMP REQUIRED

Free Books Coupon

Yes! Please rush me 4 FREE Romances and 2 FREE gifts! Please also reserve me a Reader Service subscription. If I decide to subscribe I can look forward to receiving 6 brand new Romances for just £10.80 each month, postage and packing FREE. If I decide not to subscribe I shall write to you within 10 days - I can keep the free books and gifts whatever I choose. I may cancel or suspend my subscription at any time. I am over 18 years of age.

Ms/Mrs/Miss/Mr _____ EP56R

Address _____

_____

Postcode _____ Signature _____

MPS
MAILING
PREFERENCE
SERVICE

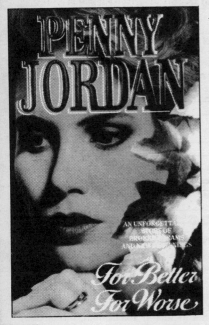

Next Month's Romances

Each month you can choose from a wide variety of romance with Mills & Boon. Below are the new titles to look out for next month, why not ask either Mills & Boon Reader Service or your Newsagent to reserve you a copy of the titles you want to buy – just tick the titles you would like and either post to Reader Service or take it to any Newsagent and ask them to order your books.

Please save me the following titles:	Please tick	√
DAWN SONG	Sara Craven	
FALLING IN LOVE	Charlotte Lamb	
MISTRESS OF DECEPTION	Miranda Lee	
POWERFUL STRANGER	Patricia Wilson	
SAVAGE DESTINY	Amanda Browning	
WEST OF BOHEMIA	Jessica Steele	
A HEARTLESS MARRIAGE	Helen Brooks	
ROSES IN THE NIGHT	Kay Gregory	
LADY BE MINE	Catherine Spencer	
SICILIAN SPRING	Sally Wentworth	
A SCANDALOUS AFFAIR	Stephanie Howard	
FLIGHT OF FANTASY	Valerie Parv	
RISK TO LOVE	Lynn Jacobs	
DARK DECEIVER	Alex Ryder	
SONG OF THE LORELEI	Lucy Gordon	
A TASTE OF HEAVEN	Carol Grace	

If you would like to order these books in addition to your regular subscription from Mills & Boon Reader Service please send £1.80 per title to: Mills & Boon Reader Service, Freepost, P.O. Box 236, Croydon, Surrey, CR9 9EL, quote your Subscriber No:.................................... (If applicable) and complete the name and address details below. Alternatively, these books are available from many local Newsagents including W.H.Smith, J.Menzies, Martins and other paperback stockists from 3 December 1993.

Name:..

Address:...

....Post Code:...........................

To Retailer: If you would like to stock M&B books please contact your regular book/magazine wholesaler for details.

You may be mailed with offers from other reputable companies as a result of this application. If you would rather not take advantage of these opportunities please tick box ☐